THINGS

THAT DON'T BELONG IN THE LIGHT

A Collection of Short Fiction

THINGS
THAT DON'T BELONG IN THE LIGHT
A Collection of Short Fiction

Matt Starr

A
Grinning Skull Press
Publication

P.O. Box 67
Bridgewater, MA 02324

Acknowledgments

Thank you:

Edgar Allan Poe, the original sad boy of American letters. Jae Stein-
bacher and Dr. Robert Bateman. The hailstorm of '97, and the Winnie
the Pooh that got me through it. Nathan Ballingrud and Cormac Mc-
Carthy. Hurricane Hugo. My sleep paralysis demon. Erich Cain. The
Macho Man Randy Savage and Manfred Mann's Earth Band. Norton,
Virginia. Funkadelic, especially George Clinton, who deserves a statue in
Kannapolis. Grinning Skull Press. My mama and them. North Carolina.
The bashful boys. My beautiful dog children. The late Charles Emery
Starr. My amazing fiancee, Emily.

I couldn't have done it without you.

TABLE OF CONTENTS

A Word:... 1

Debris.. 3

The Suffering of Jolie Bell... 17

The Light on the Other Side of the Crawl Space...................... 36

riverkeeper... 53

False Awakenings.. 73

Devil Like You 89

Another Runner in the Night.. 112

March on Carthage 127

Copperheads... 144

I was not offended.. 156

About the Author... 181

A Word:

The beautiful thing about childhood is that everything is fresh. When you're experiencing an emotion for the first time, it's more meaningful, more intense. Love, heartache, wonderment, curiosity, and especially, fear.

As a kid, the things I considered myself scared of were those I could see and touch—things like storms and spiders, the usual subjects that people fear in their youth. Growing up, I remember we had this little deck that extended from the back of our mill house in Kannapolis, North Carolina. It seemed to devour stray baseballs and basketballs, season after season, without fail, like the maw of some Homeric beast. But no matter how many of my toys I lost to that deck, I refused to crawl beneath it to retrieve anything. It wasn't because I was particularly creeped out by what I knew was under there—dead leaves, empty propane tanks, a beach chair or two—but rather because I was terrified of what I *didn't* know was under there inhabiting that darkness. What I *couldn't* know.

The older I got, the more that childhood fear mutated into an internal dread of the abstract and intangible: thoughts and concepts that went deeper than flesh and blood and couldn't be as easily understood. Psychological demons like guilt, trauma, depression, grief, and addiction superseded those visible monsters from the past. The emotional toll of life's natural devastation proved infinitely scarier than anything material. It wasn't until recently that I realized all of the aforementioned, both the knowable and unknowable, exist in the same space. Don't they?

What could be more frightening than that?

Poe once said, "Words have no power to impress the mind without the exquisite horror of their reality," and I think he was right. The ten stories in this collection toe the line between the physical and the metaphysical, the straightforward and the mysterious. It is the overlapping reality that gives life to the horror within. And so a central question prevails, then. What should we be more afraid of: the things we allow to remain hidden or the things we keep in plain sight?

Debris

Ollie was in a new place every week. Sometimes twice a week. This time, he was rowing through a leafy maze of bonelike stalks, the clouds above him a grand production of hellish green. The tornado behind him was an upside-down trapezoid in the sky, welding the ether to the ground in murderous black matrimony. Circling, circling, it was coming right at him. And it was taking its sweet time.

He riffled through the vegetation as fast as his arms and legs would afford, though he knew it was useless. The storm was gaining on him, its wail a deafening *whish*. Like sticking your ear to a shell that houses the world's largest, most troubled sea. Ollie threw a glance over his shoulder, and at once, that wall of shadowy, rotating terror filled the entirety of his visual plane. He crouched down where he was, interlaced his fingers behind his head, opened his mouth.

But in a tornado, not even God can hear you scream.

Within seconds, he was hurled into the air, the weightless feeling of freefall slinking into his gut and spreading outward. At that moment, he was reduced to human shrapnel, thrown through space, and any light he had ever known was cupped into darkness by the hands of some phenomenon beyond comprehension.

Ollie shot up in bed and keened like a raven in a graveyard. His heart was a Cherokee drum, his skin a Slip 'N Slide.

3

"What's the matter?" Justin asked, rushing in from some other part of the house, seizing Ollie by the shoulders.

Ollie peered out the bedside window, where the cool and easy green of the late Vermont spring unfurled for an immeasurable distance. "Fuck," he said, expending a heavy breath.

"Another one?" Justin said.

Ollie confirmed with a nod and brushed his clammy hand across his boyfriend's bearded cheek.

Justin knew that his partner had nightmares about tornadoes, but he didn't know why. Ollie reckoned it was too early in the relationship to unpack all of that onto him.

"What's your therapist say when you tell her about them?"

Ollie smiled. "Therapist things." He threw his legs over his side of the bed and had no more than cast the sheets aside when his phone vibrated on the nightstand. He picked it up, punched in his passcode.

The text was from his mother: *You better come I think it's the one.*

Ollie sighed and felt his eyes roll backward in his head. The "one" she referred to was the illness that would presumably take her life after a long period of declining health. As far as Ollie was concerned, she was always one breath away from "the one." But she was far more liable to outlive them all. He dismissed the ominous message and returned his phone to the nightstand.

"Your mom?" Justin asked.

"However did you know?"

"Well, aren't you gonna call her?"

Ollie crawled forward on the mattress. "Later," he said. He kissed Justin and pulled him back into bed.

A few hours later, Ollie received another phone call, but this one wasn't from his mother. This one was from a palliative care hospital in Hugo, Missouri—his hometown. The nurse on the other end of the line informed him that his mother was, in fact, in the final days of her

4

life. She had been admitted two days prior, and the prospects of her returning home weren't favorable.

The next day, Ollie boarded a flight to St. Louis. Once he landed, he drove the remainder of the way—roughly two and a half hours—in a rental car. Justin had offered to come, but Ollie protested. They weren't on that level yet. Besides, he wanted to do this himself. He felt like he *needed* to do this himself.

When he crossed into Hugo from the pastoral landscape of northeastern Missouri, a surge of nostalgia cycled through the gamut of his senses. First, the grayness of sight. Then that stale odor. The bitter nothingness of sound, taste, and touch. He hadn't seen this place since he left fifteen years before. It was a conservative, little drive-through burb, thirty miles from the Illinois state line, barely worthy of a dot on the map, and it hadn't changed a bit. The town was all fragments and bones. Like a charnel house. There were people and places, but the soul was gone. Carried off in the sky and dropped down somewhere else.

Ollie stopped at a red light and surveyed the downtown area, split into two strips of various retailers by the main road. The tailor. The hardware store. A bank with an obscure name. A building with a sign out front that said: "Dunkin Donuts coming soon!" But in the blink of Ollie's eyes, everything was rended to rubble there in the bare daylight, his personal empire of dirt and wreckage. Two-by-fours and brick and insulation. Flat and random under the sun like the contents of a child's messy room.

He closed his eyes and kept them closed. Only when he heard a honk from behind him did he open them. The stoplight was green, and the structures around him were back to normal.

"Calm your horses," he said to the driver behind him, offering a customary wave. "My bad."

He carried on to the Golden Shores Hospice House, a depressing and sterile off-white thing just down the way from the post office and the CrossFit gym. It didn't even try to mask the fact that its residents were there to die. What was the point? Ollie parked the car out front and entered the building.

"I'm looking for Norma Ellstrom," Ollie told the receptionist at the front.

She checked her chart and handed him off to a nurse, who escorted him to Room 27.

He tapped on the half-open door and pushed it the rest of the way, preparing himself for whatever might be on the other side of it. His mother was a bloated husk. She lay in bed watching her programs, inflamed yet lank limbs extruding from her paunchy torso. Thatches of hair were missing from the front of her scalp. It was hard to fathom that she was not yet seventy years old. He had gotten used to a lot of things in his life, but seeing her like this would never be one of them.

"Hey, darling," she said to Ollie, as though she had only seen him the day before.

"Hey, Mama," he replied. He dipped down and hugged her neck. Then he leaned back against the wall and crossed his arms.

Her attention returned to the television—a show about little people.

"So, what's going on this time?" Ollie asked. He still wasn't convinced that she was as ill as she claimed to be.

"I'm dying," she said plainly.

"Is that so?"

"Yeah."

"From what?"

"I went to the emergency room out yonder a couple nights ago with the godawfulest pain in my groin. They ran me through their machines, and it turns out I have an aneurysm in the artery around my hip. You know, the one they replaced that night all them years ago."

He knew the one.

"Well, anyway," she continued, waving her hand weakly. "That ain't the damndest part."

He let her continue.

"The aneurysm is all caught up on the screw they put in, and it's infected."

"What can they do?"

"Nothing. They wanna operate on it, but I told them I've had enough surgeries for this lifetime. Only thing they can do now is dope me up with painkillers and let the infection take its course."

"And you're okay with that?"

"I just said I was, didn't I?"

For a split second, Ollie saw her as she had been on that May morning in 1994. Tall and pretty. Solid. Hands that looked like they could siphon all the love and beauty from the world and put that goodness into anyone who needed it. Her presence a shape of incandescence in the formless, overcast day, her lifeforce steady as the plains are long.

"Don't you think we oughta take you to a better hospital to get a second opinion?" he asked. "Maybe out in Hannibal or St. Louis?"

"No need," she said. "I've lost my will to live. I'm ready to be with your dad. Have been for a long time."

"I know."

She changed the subject: "You ain't missing any work to be here with me, are you?"

"No, Mama," he said. "I freelance now, remember?"

While she was thinking about that, the doctor wandered into the room. He was an antique of a man with creased earlobes and flimsy, liver-spotted skin. He didn't look like he was too many years away from being in here himself. "How we doing, Normie?" he said, flashing two rows of teeth discolored by sixty years of coffee drinking.

"I'd gripe, but it wouldn't do no good," she answered.

"I'm gonna steal your boy here for a second, and then I'm gonna be back to check on you. Is that okay?"

"Yessir."

The doctor threw his arm around Ollie's neck and walked him out into the hall. "You got any questions for me, son?"

Ollie thought it over. "You sure she's of sound mind and body to make this kind of decision? She seems a little off."

Doc cleared his throat. "Well, she's on a good amount of hydromorphone to keep her comfortable. She'll be right loopy and lethargic 'til she goes."

"How long?"

The doctor's smile waned. "Fast. Two weeks. We've cut off the antibiotics at her request."

The finality of the implications caught hold of Ollie's throat, and he felt a tear crop up in his eye.

"Now, now, son. She's made it longer than she probably should have. Y'all are both living on borrowed time. Hell, we all are."

Ollie squinted. "Pardon me?"

"She told me y'all were here when it happened. I was, too. It'll be twenty-four years tomorrow. Ain't that something?" He traced the corners of his mouth with his thumb and pointer finger, remembering. "I rode it out in the basement. I was surprised anyone was still alive when I came up. I've never seen such violence done onto people like that, and I've been in a war."

The sound of a failing heartbeat on a monitor down the hall rang into the corridor. But it quickly became something else.

It was the middle of the night when the siren fired up, a winding boomerang of sound that moaned with an unworldly sorrow. Ollie was nine years old. He sprang out of bed, t-shirt to his knees. His mother shivered sleep from her shoulders as she walked barefoot to the front door. His father was working the graveyard shift at the stockyard. There had been rain and a few rumbles, a thunderstorm to the north, but nothing more.

Warning sirens sounded from time to time; that's just what they did around here. But little ever materialized from them. One could assume as much from the way Ollie's mother acted, watching the night from behind the storm door like someone might watch a bird at a porchside feeder.

"What's going on, Mama?" Ollie asked in his small voice.

"Nothing, baby," she said. "Go back to bed."

Thunder came not long after her last word, and it had weight to it that Ollie had never felt before. An unsettling quiet followed, the emptiness of which nearly made him ill. He balled the hem of his t-shirt with his fists.

Something wasn't right.

Thunder growled again, then lightning flashed. Then they saw it. A massive wedge funnel backlit by a sheet of pale light on the horizon. A monster from a silent black-and-white movie. Something coming for them in the dark. Any hope that it had been a trick of the eye was extinguished by another flash.

Ollie's mother gasped.

He had been scared plenty before, but hearing that sound from her, that hiss, was the first time he'd ever tasted fear in his mouth.

She turned. "Get in the closet," she ordered.

They filed into the coat closet in the hallway, and she turtled over him.

He was crying now.

"Please, Lord, let it pass," she pleaded. "Heavenly Father, let it miss us."

No one was listening.

The sound started in the distance but swelled closer and higher at a rate that was unnerving in its slowness. Building over several minutes like pressure in a tank. It was far away, and then it was less far away, and then it was near, and then it was upon them—the finger of God. Rooting through the landscape, leaving nothing unturned, little spared. Ollie had heard people describe it as a rolling freighter or a jet engine, but that wasn't accurate to him. No, it was more like a barrage of rushing water, each droplet sharp and impossible. A sensory overload. The sheerest of energies. Nothing of the Earth could be this loud. The windows shattered as projectiles began to beat against the house. Boards, metal scraps, bones picked of their meat. Ollie knew that his mother was howling, but he couldn't hear her. Which meant he also couldn't hear the outer wall buckling and folding away.

As the tornado went overhead, the ceiling vanished and Ollie could see the column of ravaged ghosts rising in a chorus of screams above him. Mutants in a strange new world of cataclysm. He knew some of them were children like him, and he wondered what their names were. But they were gone. Cottony pink insulation rained down in their wake. An interior wall collapsed onto his mother's back and pinned her against him in a squatted position.

The commotion died down, not all at once but close. Mere seconds later, it was over. In the eerie calm that followed, a moist warmth collected in Ollie's crotch. He had pissed himself.

"Are you okay, darling?" his mother asked, strained and out of breath.

"I think so."

"I can't move," she grunted. "I'm trapped under the wall. Can you wiggle free?"

He tried. "No."

"All right, we gotta holler, okay?"

"Yes, ma'am," Ollie sniffled.

So they did. They shouted until they were hoarse. Until they heard sirens almost two hours later. They were different kinds of sirens, but they still filled Ollie's heart with overwhelming despair.

A prominent meteorologist would later refer to the tornado as "'unsurvivable' above ground." But they had survived it. Sixty-six other people hadn't been so lucky.

When Ollie had turned eighteen and was old enough to go out on his own, he researched places that had the least amount of tornadic activity in the country. That's how he wound up in New England. He never thought he would see Hugo again, but here he was.

It was dinnertime at Golden Shores, and a tray of food sat on his mother's bedside table. A woeful arrangement of dry-looking grilled chicken, green beans, and mashed potatoes. Another show was on the television, this one about the morbidly obese. Ollie's mother wallowed in discomfort, her long legs kneading the blanket into the mattress. She was getting fussy.

"You okay?" Ollie asked.

She grimaced toward the plate of food. "I'm so weak," she said. "Feed me, Oliver."

He grabbed the spoon, scooped a corner off of the mashed potatoes. He held it to her mouth.

She craned her head in a pitiful display and took a bite. She rolled the potatoes around in her open mouth, a shadowperson unlearned of her basic manners and processes. Unlearned of her humanity. She started to cry.

It hurt Ollie deeply. "What's the matter?" he asked.

"Look at me," she said. "Laying here like a fucking baby. Shit in my britches. Can't even feed myself."

He was taken aback by this. His mother had never been much for cursing when he was younger. He assured himself that it was the painkillers and continued his sonly duty. He fed her one bite. Then another. Her weeping all the while, eyes and nose running. Food tumbling down her chin and onto her bib.

A wave of anxiety mounted within him, and he resorted to the only way he knew how to cope: He had to get out. "I'm gonna go get some fresh air," he said. "I'll be right back."

"Don't leave."

"I'll be right back," he repeated.

She mewled faintly behind him as he left the room and powerwalked toward the Exit sign at the end of the wing. But there was a sound that stopped him halfway there. It was a beseeching whisper coming from Room 33. The door was open, but it was full dark inside.

Ollie stepped into the doorway and flipped on the dim light. "Hello?"

The quarters appeared normal upon first glance: a television, a bed, a window. But then a man slithered out from under the bed, his body squelching on the tile floor. He was waxen as a cavefish, and everything below the waist was gone—save a medusa of entrails that painted the ground oily red in his wake.

He set his eyes upon Ollie and smiled. "Lucky I took cover!"

"Christ!" Ollie yelled, jumping back, almost falling.

The man wobbled forward on the heels of his hands.

Ollie nearly tripped as he tore for the Exit sign. Once outside, he paced off into the evening, on the verge of hyperventilation, and whipped out his phone to text Justin. But an object caught the corner of his eye before he could open his messaging app. Just beyond the sidewalk, a woman hung from a denuded tree limb like something skewered. Her body was in Pallor Mortis, and a corona of blood traversed her head.

With a hand over his mouth, Ollie ran away from her. Further down the road, another man lay mangled against a bus stop like a science experiment gone awry. A white, calcified shard protruded from his disfigured neck. As Ollie passed him, the man sang: "My thigh bone's connected to my hip bone. My hip bone's connected to my neck bone. Wait. That's not right. Whoops!"

It was then that Ollie launched into a full sprint. There, in the middle of the street ahead, a commune of wraiths gathered by starlight, tribal and aimless in their movements. The wet heat of the night had called these dead to dance, the winds they were born from so violent that all the hair had been removed from their naked bodies. The people chanted in sirenlike tones, and Ollie wrapped his fingers around his own face and cried out.

"You're imagining this," he said. "It's not real!"

But that's not how trauma works. Trauma moves slow and upward until the house implodes, and only a slab foundation remains. It has a way of staying with a place. It has a way of staying with a person, too. Ollie knew that. Every time the sky darkened with clouds, he had to practice breathing techniques. Until he was twenty-five years old, he would find refuge in the nearest closet during thunderstorms. Whenever he was searching for a new place to live, he refused to consider anything on the second floor or higher.

It was real to him.

He tried to push it way down as he walked back to Golden Shores, got in his car, and drove to the motel.

His room wasn't nice, but he had been in worse. It was what you could expect for forty-nine dollars a night. He didn't sleep much, and when the morning came, he skipped the complimentary continental breakfast and headed straight for the hospital, hoping to try again. The air was humid, and the atmosphere was ripe for afternoon thunderstorms. It made Ollie nervous.

At Golden Shores, his mother's spirits seemed to be somewhat improved.

"I'm sorry about last night," Ollie said to her. "I don't know what got into me."

"I honestly don't remember much of it," she admitted. "It gets worse at night, and the medicine makes me a little loony."

"I'll try to do better."

"You done good for what you were handed," she said.

He squeezed her hand, feeling himself grow emotional, remembering that endless night, what it had been like in the debris, her dislocated hip wrapped around him. It was so hard to let go. He watched television with her until she finished her lunch.

"Can I get you anything?" he asked.

"My mouth is awful dry," she said. "Will you get me some hard candy?"

"You bet," he said. He grabbed his keys, kissed her on the forehead.

The general store was within walking distance, so Ollie went for an afternoon stroll as the sun slipped in and out of rain-plumped clouds. The building was just as he remembered it—albeit less lively—with old-timey soda bottle coolers, glass cases, and buckets of candy that you wouldn't find most places anymore. He bagged some peppermint and butterscotch and went to the front counter.

"Afternoon," a lady with a smoker's voice greeted from the other side. She was ancient and doughy, and her hair was a hedgerow of blinding white.

"How's it going?" Ollie said, casting a glance around the store. "You don't seem terribly busy today."

"Oh, you won't find a lot of people out around here today," she said absently.

"That so?"

She keyed in his candy. "Yeah. Something bad happened on this day several years back."

The word "bad" hung in the air between them. Ollie pretended not to know what she was talking about.

"Twister. F5. Worst one in state history 'til Joplin."

He handed her the money, took the candy. "I'm sorry."

She stared past him. Through him. "Might as well have been yesterday. Weather radio went to showing its ass in the dead of night, and it weren't five, ten minutes before the sucker jumped on us. Goddamn thing squashed my sister like a bug. Sucked up the house she was in, but then up and dropped another one on top of her. That's what it does, you know?" She leaned in close. "It eats people. Things, too. Swallows them up in its belly. But it don't take them nowhere. Not really. I was in my bathtub screaming, 'Holy Hannah.' Bastard took my dogs, shredded one of them like a damn cheese grater, but it spared me. Most days, I wish it woulda been the other way around."

The last syllable had barely escaped her lips when the Edison bulbs winked and dimmed overhead. Then they went out altogether. There was a high sound. Like a nuclear reactor alarm or maybe a boatswain's pipe. A siren song. Invisible feet scraping against the floor. A baby crying. Scared people saying no, praying. An avalanche of wind or water, it didn't really matter. Ollie's ears popped. He breathed slow but hard, every fear receptor in his brain propelled into overdrive. The storefront windows burst, and glass scattered across the floor like knucklebones in a game of Jacks. The room shook, and Ollie could smell the putrid mercaptan in the natural gas as whatever was happening trailed off.

One by one, the lights returned.

The lady behind the counter went on like nothing had happened.

"Anyhow," she said. "Is there anything else I can help you with?"

"All right, I've gotta get the fuck outta here," Ollie said as he stormed out of the general store, the ritual complete behind him. "I've done all I can."

A pane of suffocated sun portended to the southwest, and a bizarre magnetism burdened the earth. It had begun to rain. How could he have ever thought this was a good idea?

Ollie texted Justin that he was coming back right away. He would say goodbye to his mother, what she had become. He would make sure to remember her for how she was, to keep it with him always, and then he would seek shelter. Ride it out, leave. He rushed to his motel room, and as he packed his bags, something pelted the windows. It was hail the size of marbles. Then ping pong balls. He hurried to the car, shielded himself with his jacket, and drove to the hospital, a biblical thunderstorm now bearing down on him.

He found mild relief inside, but that quickly evaporated. Golden Shores Hospice House was a ghost town. Not only did it look like nobody was there, but it looked like no one had *ever* been there.

"Hello?" he called.

An echo was the only answer.

"Hello, goddammit!"

Nothing, again.

He proceeded to Room 27, which was buried in the abyss. The television in the next room was talking in an officious voice: "This is a particularly dangerous situation, folks. A tornado emergency. Now I know that's not what anyone in Hugo wants to hear, especially today, but get to your safe place right now. A storm shelter, a basement. An interior room on the lowest level of your home."

Ollie stepped into his mother's room. The power went out.

"Mama?"

He could see her shape in the bed, but nothing else. The thunder

15

from his childhood arrived, and it pulled something else into the present with it. That boundless blitz of soundwaves being sheared, endless water filtered through a too-small drain. Lightning flickered to reveal his mother rising from the bed, coming toward him with outstretched arms. Plodding. She was the storm he couldn't weather. She was a spinning ball of pure agony.

"Feed me," she said.

He panted in horror.

"Feed me, Oliver," she repeated.

Then another voice. A throaty liquid scream from a hungry maw. "Feed me!"

The roof flew away. The walls disappeared.

"Feed me!"

He did.

The Suffering of Jolie Bell

It wasn't exactly on the way back home from her current assignment, but when Jolie Bell caught wind of the Devil's Toybox, she couldn't resist. She had just wrapped up a 3,000-word article on a haunted Victorian mansion in Mississippi—standard stuff—when she stumbled across a thread in one of the half-dozen subreddits she followed. A "hovel of horrors" (as one user had described it) behind a place the locals called Hell's Half Acre seemed right up her alley.

Jolie was a travel blogger, but not the kind to make recommendations for romantic getaways or scenic hikes through nature. She was after something grimmer: If anything bizarre or fucked-up had happened somewhere, that's where she wanted to be. Her documented experiences had amassed quite a following over the previous three years, and her ever-growing list of subscribers might as well have been the wind at her back, pushing her toward highways on the fringe of the living.

Name the place, and there's a good chance Jolie had been there. The shack of floor-to-ceiling mirrors in rural Louisiana. The abandoned church in Ohio where a cult leader convinced his entire congregation to be snakebitten to death. The burial ground for a native tribe that had been slaughtered by settlers. Now she was bound for southeastern Appalachia.

17

She crossed the North Carolina state line into a little town called Flat Rock shortly after nine o'clock in the evening. The entire area was cast in darkness, the exception being a truckstop diner off the highway. Jolie coasted into a parking spot, debating whether or not she was desperate enough to go in. The building itself looked clean and homey enough, but she couldn't help but think it was the type of place where the employees hid the sanitation score behind the potato chip rack. Still, she was hungry and figured a bit more research couldn't hurt, and so she decided to brave her doubts.

Jolie shivered as she entered the door. She did her best to ignore the three or four sets of eyes ogling her, the expressionless, tired-looking men they belonged to, and sat in a booth where she could see everything in front of her, including the sanitation rating. She had judged prematurely: It was a very respectable 98. She pulled out her laptop as the waitress approached, a little book of tickets in hand.

"How we doing tonight, Suge?" the waitress asked. Her name tag read Bonnie.

"Fine, thank you," Jolie said. "A little cold."

Bonnie laughed. "I know it. Summer turns straight to winter here. We don't get no fall no more."

"You're not the first person I've heard say that."

"Can I get you something to drink?"

"I'll take a coffee, black," Jolie said.

Bonnie fetched a full pot and ceramic mug from the bar, then returned to where Jolie sat. "We doing food tonight?" she asked as she poured a cup.

"Two eggs over-easy and bacon, please," Jolie said, glancing at the menu. "Oh, and hashbrowns."

Bonnie scribbled away. "You got it."

"You guys wouldn't happen to have Wi-Fi here, would you?"

"Afraid not," Bonnie frowned. "Sorry about that."

"That's all right," Jolie said, though she could tell she wasn't hiding her disappointment well.

Bonnie doubled back toward the kitchen. *Of course they don't have Wi-Fi,* Jolie thought. This was the only place in a ten-mile radius currently using electricity, so she guessed she probably should have been grateful for that. She considered using her phone for research, but she didn't like to strain her eyes on small screens, and she wasn't confident that she had a signal anyway. She was beginning to accept that she would probably have to continue her quest with limited knowledge.

Not much was known about the Toybox other than that it was thirty or so miles from her current location. It wasn't on the map, but there was a very specific set of instructions for how to get there. From an experiential standpoint, descriptions ranged from an Ayahuasca ceremony to the torture of war prisoners. In other words, exactly what Jolie's blog was going for. She cupped her mug with both hands and drifted into the background noise. Forks and spoons clanking on plates. Spatulas raking across a flat top grill. Crushed ice scraping up and down in cups. There was a soothing quality to it.

No more than five minutes had elapsed when Bonnie returned with Jolie's food. "Here we go," Bonnie said. "Anything else I can get you?"

"I'm fine, thanks."

"All right, then. Just give me a holler, Suge."

Suge. It puzzled Jolie that Bonnie would call her that. Southern hospitality wasn't lost on her, but it usually came from people twice as old. Bonnie seemed her age, despite the obvious motherly qualities. She looked like all the other girls Jolie had gone to high school with a dozen years before, most of whom were now involved in pyramid schemes. Jolie was mostly thankful for where she was, though she had never imagined it would be this way. As she ate, her mind wandered onto the subject of life, the different paths it takes people on. She chewed as though it were her last meal.

Bonnie returned as Jolie was taking her last bite. "All done?"

"I think so," Jolie said.

Bonnie collected the plate. Then she nodded toward Jolie's laptop, which was still on the table. "What did you need it for?"

"I'm sorry?"

"What did you need the Wi-Fi for?" Bonnie questioned. "If you don't mind me asking."

"Oh," Jolie said, trying to think of how to explain it. "It's just this thing I do. I run this blog called 'She Shall Suffer, She Shall Atone.'"

"Where'd you come up with a name like that?"

"It's an obscure reference from Mary Shelley's *Frankenstein*," Jolie answered, blushing. She came off sounding so awkward. There was a reason she preferred writing to talking.

"What's it about?"

"I visit places," Jolie said. "Strange areas or sites that are supposedly haunted. Then I write about them."

Bonnie sat the plate back down and took a seat across the booth. Her interest was apparent. "That's fascinating. You think anyone actually goes to the places you write about?"

"Some, maybe," Jolie said. "I imagine the really dedicated ones follow in my footsteps, but most people read comfortably from afar. It makes them scared without putting them in immediate danger. Makes them feel alive." She leaned in. "If you really wanna know the truth, though, most of it's bullshit. I use my imagination to make up something that sounds good. Ghosts in windows, creepy sounds. Shit like that."

Bonnie frowned. "That don't seem right. You shouldn't lie to people, least of all yourself."

"It's harmless," Jolie said, leaning back, a little ashamed.

"What's the scariest place you've ever been?"

Jolie peered into her half-drunk coffee, her nerves suddenly fired up like a car that's been sitting in the shed for months. A breath of uneasiness sank through her, made her skin feel like it was expanding. She was in the room, supine. She was on the cold floor. She was staring into the void, and then she was staring into the ceiling fan light fixture, and then she was reanimated, ripped through an electrostatic current.

"Suge?"

Jolie looked up, but the person sitting across from her wasn't Bonnie. She didn't look like Bonnie had but a moment ago, at least. She was jagged and blue-skinned, her constricted pupils heavily lidded. Her wind was shallow, and her posture was slumping by the breath.

"What's the scariest place you've ever been, Suge?" Bonnie asked again, a rattle in her chest.

Jolie turned toward the bar. A trucker shifted on a too-small stool, sipped his coffee. In the galley-style kitchen, a cook cracked some eggs onto the flat top. Something played on the jukebox. Jolie practiced her breathing, not wanting to face Bonnie but knowing she had to. Once she finally did, she saw that Bonnie was back to the way she had been. Mellow and amiable, though she seemed concerned that Jolie still hadn't answered her.

"You all right, Suge?"

Jolie could feel her face getting hot, her eyes starting to blink. She fished a twenty from her pocket and placed it on the table. "Keep the change," she said, making for the door.

Jolie did hydrocodone for the first time with her friends when she was fifteen. Margo had lifted some from her grandmother's prescription bottle, and then the four girls convened at the Wheelwright BBQ House in Old Rose Township, Pennsylvania, on a Saturday afternoon. Three of them giggled as they cupped two tabs apiece in their palms, a basket of picked-over onion rings on the table in front of them.

Alyssa was less enthusiastic. She wasn't the Jesus freak she had once been, but she was still less of a risk-taker than her girlfriends. "I don't know about this, Margo," she said.

In the next seat, Sophie rolled her eyes.

"Just take them, bitch," Margo replied in her signature antagonizing tone. "God's got more important shit to do than watch you drop downers."

Margo was a year older than the others, and they all looked up to her—especially Jolie. She was thin without trying, and she dressed the way she wanted to, and she didn't care about anything because caring wasn't cool, and she dated guys from the college up the road.

Alyssa sulked. "You don't have to be so aggressive."

Margo smirked.

Jolie had her doubts, too, but she didn't want to appear unworthy in the eyes of the others. Friends weren't easy to come by for her, and friends like Margo weren't easy to come by for *anyone*. You achieved a certain status by simply being in her presence. Jolie and Sophie were always jockeying for the position of best friend, so Jolie couldn't let the others see that she was anything less than one-hundred-percent committed.

The girls threw indiscreet glances over their shoulders to make sure no one was watching, and then they popped the pills and washed them down with their sodas. Alyssa winced at the bitter taste, the snaggy fullness in her throat. Margo, never one to be outdone, threw back two more tabs. Her tight lips cut a proud smile.

"What now?" Jolie asked.

"You'll see," Margo said.

Twenty minutes passed before Jolie did. Her brain felt like white noise, her body felt so…good. If there was another adjective for it, Jolie didn't know what it was. It was like a beautiful death, a simultaneous peak and lull of the senses. Her legs were melting into her chair.

Each of the girls wore a thousand-yard stare, and none of them spoke until Alyssa shot up and hurried toward the bathroom.

Jolie found it difficult to speak. "Maybe I should go check on her," she said.

"She's gonna yack," Margo responded with pinhole eyes. "It's normal."

It didn't feel normal to Jolie. She liked it, but it scared her—that something could create this kind of bliss. She breathed in her surroundings, a pleasant numbness spreading outward from her core. There was a flash of paranoia, too, and even that felt satisfying. Like danger.

"I'm fucked up," Sophie said.

Margo smiled wryly, looked at Jolie. "That's the point."

Jolie laid off painkillers for two years after that day with her friends. She had enjoyed the high but not the emptiness that followed. If the mood struck, she opted for booze or the occasional hit off a joint instead. Then she tore her ACL in a lacrosse match her senior year, and her doctor prescribed the same thing Margo had given her at the restaurant. In its own twisted way, it was almost like destiny.

Jolie used the hydrocodone responsibly at first while she recovered from knee surgery: one or two tablets every four to six hours as needed for acute pain. But after a while, the effects became underwhelming. She began to add an extra one here, one there, and before she knew it, she was doubling up. The feeling became a companion—warm and comforting when it was there, sorely missed when it wasn't. The interim between doses was a loneliness supreme.

A month and a half after her procedure, Jolie's doctor ended her prescription. That was the first time she became wise to her mortality, the impermanence of her own flesh. The withdrawals were murder. The body clenching, the sleeplessness, the racing heart, the scaries, the runs. She cried like she hadn't since she was a baby, and in her mind, there was only one person who could make it stop.

Margo had gone off to college in the fall, but she still had connections in Old Rose Township, and she was more than willing to introduce them to Jolie. These were the days before the tight laws and the DEA crackdowns. There was a whole network of dealers and buyers, runners and patients. Some of the physicians were in on it, too. Some of the local police. An epidemic through smalltown America.

Jolie used any means necessary to avoid dope-sickness: stealing, forging, and once or twice, sexual favors. Once she graduated high school, it only seemed natural for her to room with her bestie, Margo, despite her parents' reservations. Margo had found herself on academic probation in short order, and whispers of her lifestyle had reached home. Nonetheless, Jolie joined her friend at school, and the two of them became the sisters neither of them ever had. They graduated from hydrocodone to oxycodone, only hung out with other users. Over time, Jolie distanced herself from her real family.

Margo finished her sophomore year but didn't re-enroll for the following semester. Jolie dropped out a year and a half later. She was growing isolated, anxious and depressed, disgusted with her own body and the woman she had become. But she also had problems that were even more distressing: With no financial aid to fall back on, she didn't have the funds to pay rent, let alone get her fix.

On a particularly agonizing night, she crossed the hall to Margo's room, nose running, blanket wrapped about her shoulders. She knocked, but there was no answer. Feeling the doorknob turn in her hand, she let herself in. The bedroom, which displayed a mess fit for a hoarder, was ill-lit. Margo sat on a futon by the window, a girl of ninety-five pounds soaking wet with her eyes closed and her chin in her chest.

"Margo," Jolie said. Her words were all throat and no teeth. She was hoarse for no reason.

The girl didn't budge.

"Margo," Jolie repeated, this time nudging her friend on the shoulder.

Margo breathed in like she had never tasted oxygen. Her head was slow to rise, and when her cloudy eyes flitted open and caught the light, they resembled gutter-bound glass bottles. Once she realized she was conscious, she offered up a sardonic smile. "What the fuck happened to knocking?" she asked.

"I did," Jolie said.

"Okay, well, why are you interrupting my beauty sleep?" She scratched her sleeved arm; she only wore long-sleeved shirts now, even in the summer.

Jolie heard the question, but she didn't hear it at the same time. She was adrift in the sight of Margo, like she was laying eyes on her for the first time in many years. Margo had never been big in terms of physical stature, but her presence had always been ineliminable, contagious. Her confidence had been polarizing, whether it had come from misplaced insecurity or natural aplomb, but now she was an afterthought of a person. She was disappearing. Jolie found it devastatingly sad.

"Helloooo?" Margo said.

"Do you have any Roxies?" Jolie asked.

"You out?"

"Yeah."

Margo affected the face she always made when she was up to no good; then she paused, as though she were considering something very delicate through the gray in her mind. She reached for the drawer of the end table next to her and opened it. "I don't have any Roxies," she said. "But I might have something better."

Jolie watched as her friend laid a sheaf of foil on the end table. The substance within was a pale brown powder.

Jolie was northbound at the first indication of dawn. Visibility was low, so she passed the last two notable landmarks—a country club and a Montessori school—at a virtual crawl. The fog coagulated across the mountainscape like a silver bisque. It was so thick, even, that she nearly missed her contact point after three miles of hardwood wilderness.

The blackboard tree at the fringe of the Pisgah National Forest was unmistakable amidst the towering overgrowth of ash, cedar, and pine. Indigenous to the southern and eastern hemispheres of the world, the species had no biological reason for being here. But it was. And it was thriving.

Jolie parked in a carpet of dead leaves and killed the engine. She checked her rearview mirror before exiting the car, a habit, and what she saw bottomed out her stomach with dread, prickled her arms and legs with raised flesh: Margo lay across the backseat, both arms freckled with track marks, a red-tinted froth bubbling from her lips. She was staring at Jolie with fixed eyes. The eyes of a child.

Jolie instinctively began to run through her breathing exercises. Then she shifted her focus toward herself in the mirror. A thread of blood wormed out of her right nostril and headed for her upper lip. She raked the back of her hand across her face to clean it but saw no evidence of residue when she looked down. When her eyes returned to the mirror, the blood was gone. So was Margo. Jolie drank in the momentary relief, but it was swiftly replaced by the expectation of the next episode. Sometimes, she wished she could turn her brain off.

She opened the car door. The perfume of the blackboard tree hit her from across the road. It was spicy and inebriating, toeing the line between rotten and saccharine. And its reach was total. As she neared it, Jolie found herself transfixed by its curious features: It had an ungainly, lenticel-striped trunk from which sap bled like milk, and its still-green, larva-like flowers snowballed from semi-elliptical leaves. Its branches opened upward like a hand unto God. It was a true marvel of nature, a chilling splash of color amongst the black and white.

Jolie tried not to be distracted by it. She remembered why she was there and pressed on. Hell's Half Acre had been another world around the time of the railroad's arrival in the late nineteenth century. Shops, storefronts, and bars had occupied this lot of land in those prosperous days, but sin, violence, debauchery, and specifically illegal liquor gradually made a home there. It wasn't long after an outlaw killed five keepers of the peace in a shootout—before turning the gun on himself—that the area folded, and the forest reclaimed it.

Now the place was populated by trees and trees alone. Jolie searched for the symbols that were said to mark them, runic characters tattooed into the bark. Six letters in total would carve the way. She discovered the first on the back of a tree to her right: an upward-pointing arrow known as *teiwaz*. The next was *othilia*, which resembled a vertical diamond with stick legs; Jolie located it just ahead.

The most difficult symbol to hunt down was *jera*, a figure represented by two oppositely faced chevrons that ran almost parallel to one another. It was crudely etched into a dying ash about twenty trees to the left. *Berkana*, a capital "B" composed of two sideways triangles, shortly followed. Then another *othilia*. As she plunged deeper into the woods, Jolie realized that there was no sound here. No limbs crackling and falling to the earth below, no animals skittering about. The air around her was weightless and fatigued, an utterly spiritless ecosystem. It didn't feel possible.

Jolie was fully immersed in the forest when she came upon the letter "Y" with a vertical line through the middle—*algiz*. Questions swarmed her mind as she palpated the engraving a quarter of the way up the pine tree. How long had these symbols been here? Was someone responsible for maintaining them? What was it about this place that made it feel interposed between Heaven and Hell? She surveyed her surroundings, paranoid in a way she hadn't been to this point. Only the gray stared back at her.

There was one more thing Jolie had to do, though she was skeptical about it, to say the least. It necessitated a considerable devotion to superstition, for which she had never had much use.

Nevertheless, she spoke the words into the universe, each letter caught in a spiral of smoke: "When the light of the day has gone away, the Devil will come out of his house to play."

It sounded ridiculous and creepy, this nursery rhyme, but the instructions were clear. She needed to recite it two more times. She studied the inscribed *algiz* again. Was it more profound, more legible than it had been before?

Jolie rattled off the phrase again: "When the light of the day has gone away, the Devil will come out of his house to play. When the light of the day has gone away, the Devil will come out of his house to play."

In the immediate aftermath, there was nothing. But then there was a sound that was born as a thought; in Jolie's ears, it grew into a whisper. She couldn't be sure, but she believed she heard the twinkling tune of a wind-up music box, dancing atop the air on soft, antique feet. It was something from the old country, a grandparent's bedroom, a shutoff area of a bric-a-brac store.

Straight ahead, behind a row of sickly pines, sat a shabby wooden building with a rust-bitten tin roof. Nothing had occupied that space a moment ago, Jolie was sure of it, but now the structure peered back as though it had been there a hundred years, witnessed a hundred trees tumble to the end of their life cycle. It threw off a distinctive odor, even from a significant distance. The odor of the blackboard tree. It resembled a large lean-to, a life-size toybox. The Devil's Toybox.

Jolie refused to shoot up, so she never considered herself a junkie. That's what she told herself, at least. Snorting the dope made the whole situation more palatable. Margo, on the other hand, wouldn't take it any other way. The end of the belt looked like a limp snake between her still-pretty teeth as she tightened the buckle at the bottom of her bicep, something yearning, aching in her eyes. Once she located a ripe vein, she flicked the syringe and licked the needle before driving it into her bulging flesh. Scarlet mingled with brown. She kicked the plunger, and the black seal fell as the liquid mixture was dispatched. The effect was almost instantaneous.

Margo was famous for saying that she could quit whenever she wanted, but the mask of sedation she now wore didn't look like it belonged to someone who had a choice in the matter.

A sufficient line of her own awaited Jolie on the coffee table, and she didn't leave it wanting. She insufflated the dirty powder, slow and methodical in her way, careful to leave no residue behind. The presentation of the familiar burn followed, as did the vinegary taste, the gritty postnasal drip. The euphoria, a balmy and drowsy phenomenon, coursed through her face, her body. Heroin was much more affordable than the pills, much easier to score. How had she ever existed without it?

Both girls looked at each other, spacey, loose; it was hard to hold a thought, hard to feel anything other than the duality of sensory overload and sensory nullification. Their nightly ritual observed, there was nothing left to do but enjoy the ride, weather the comedown, and look forward to the next trip. It was Margo who succumbed to the high first. She slipped out of consciousness and slumped backward on the futon. Jolie didn't think anything of it at first: Nodding was just part of the game. But then she studied Margo's chest. It wasn't rising or falling.

A spasm of muted panic shot through Jolie's blissful paralysis. She stood, which was more of a chore than it normally was, and had a mind to go tend to her friend. The gathering attack stopped any of those intentions cold. Jolie was all at once immobile, weak. She said Margo's name, but it sounded like it came from a third party. Even through the internal clutter, Jolie could tell that something was wrong. She pulled out her phone. The last thing she remembered was hitting the emergency icon before she surrendered to the gray blindness.

It was there. Jolie couldn't *actually* believe it was there. The more she gazed upon the Toybox, the more it looked like an afterthought of an extinct place. A thing that time forgot. The jingle in the air continued to graze about her ears as she approached the building, windowless and misshapen. Once she was close enough to touch it, she held her hand an inch away from the surface. A dull heat radiated from the veiny grooves in the wood, and with it, the blackboard tree's stink. Second thoughts cropped up in her head, but she knew they wouldn't do her any good. She knew, down to her bones, that it was already too late to turn around. She tugged at the front door, and it creaked open.

A wall of depressurization hit Jolie as soon as she stepped inside and shut the door. Her body responded with the slightest notions of fatigue and nausea, but they weren't unbearable. The interior of the Toybox, a poky single room with a low ceiling, was bathed in natural light despite the absence of windows. It was sterile and immaculate, a far cry from what the outside suggested. It reminded Jolie of rehab.

Her eyes wandered every corner of the bare room until they detected its lone object: a bulbous steel tank situated on the matte floor directly in front of her. If it had been a snake, it would have bitten her. To the average person, this contraption may have been a mystery, but Jolie immediately recognized it as an early version of a sensory deprivation chamber.

This was the mysterious experiential aspect of the Devil's Toybox—the part of the equation that had a way of evading the message boards.

Jolie appraised it with a kind of blurred awe. Generally speaking, these devices were utilized for their therapeutic properties: The objective of the game was to lay atop the water within, where isolation and flotation would strip one from the threads of the external world. Jolie had never used one, but the result was said to be nothing short of resurrective and transcendent.

She had a feeling there was something different about this one, though. It seemed to taunt her as her symptoms of malaise worsened. A cold turkey kind of reaction with which she was all too familiar. She couldn't wrap her mind around the suspicion that a wordless voice was speaking to her. It was beckoning her, telling her that the tank would make it all better, make it all go away. She was a slave to it in that moment. Through the cloudiness, Jolie managed a little reason. This was a sketchy situation, sure, but she hadn't come all this way for nothing. Besides, nothing was scarier than what she had been through. Of that much, she was certain.

Jolie took two cautious steps forward and lifted the lid of the tank; it opened like the mouth of a giant clam. The hollow innards of the chamber, clean and well-kept, held a bath of still water that must have measured nearly a foot in depth. Jolie dipped a finger beneath the surface and found the temperature warm and agreeable—damn-near identical to the feel of her own skin.

The maundering voice continued to lure her.

She gave it what it wanted. Without further deliberation, Jolie removed her clothes. Her knit hat, her jacket and sweatshirt, her jeans and boots and socks. She was down to her underwear, standing there in the Devil's Toybox, but she wasn't cold. The supernatural fever of this place had softened her faculties. She stepped into the tank, one foot and then the other, and lowered herself into the water. The contact was a delight to the nerve endings. With one last whole-body breath, she pulled down on the handle attached to the lid, encasing herself in a death-like darkness. She lay on her back, floating, suspended in what seemed like boundless space. After a minute or two, she was overcome by sightlessness and the nonexistence of sound. Her concept of smell abandoned her next, and then her ability to feel altogether.

The final seconds of this conscious state were marked by a moment of clarity like she'd had in the woods. Why the *fuck* had she gotten in here? She had made some terrible mistakes in the past, but this might rival them all. This chamber was in working order, which must have meant someone was responsible for the upkeep. Why would she so willingly put herself at their mercy? How could she be so stupid?

She had precious little time to answer these questions.

Her point of view was from the ground, discarnate, but as if her back were flat against the laminate floor, and then she was on the ceiling, seeing it all from the crown molding of the corner. Then she was back on the ground again. Not quite inside herself this time, but close by. A bodiless visitor returning to the scene. The room before her existed in a panorama of cyan and heavy shadows, and she could see it so plainly. Lopsided furniture and potato chip bags and random articles of clothing and miscellaneous paraphernalia. The futon. Margo. Her former self, like a strange clone. Something deeper than fear, rawer, got the better of Jolie as this phantasm became reality.

She had come back to the place of her nightmares for sport. There were three contestants: Jolie the Visitor, Jolie the Former, and Margo.

Jolie Bell the Visitor was fixed in her paralysis. It felt as though weights were hanging from her, suspended beneath the floorboards by hooks in her skin. An unseen force determined to drag her kicking into Hell—if she *could* kick. Fact was, she couldn't do anything except watch it play out as it had a thousand times in her dreams. But this sequel was more terrifying than usual. There was something beyond the optics waiting for her if she didn't pull through. It tasted her, deemed her appetizing. Jolie wanted to scream every last tear from her body.

The girls had fallen victim to a hot dose. It happened all the time: Dealers would lace their heroin with a potent synthetic called fentanyl to dig the spikes in, have their customers coming back for more. But none of them were chemists; they almost always added too much. Now

Jolie the Former and Margo were racing against an invisible clock, two contestants in a rigged game, two overdosed girls primed for the Obituaries. Could Jolie the Visitor help them?

A few beats came and went, each fainter than the last. Jolie the Visitor knew she was slipping away, slipping closer to her cold body, her former self, but it wasn't calm and peaceful. The seconds were filled with a gutting dismay, an utter helplessness that surpassed anything Jolie could have ever imagined. She was marching to the end of a ledge without feet.

Jolie the Visitor, the Immaterial, was now fully rejoined with her physical body, Jolie the Former, supine, reunited to die. She was sure that she was at the end of the line when the thuds arrived, reverberating through her mind like ominous clock chimes. Two paramedics barged into the room with their jump bags at the ready. One, an older, heavyset man, tended to Jolie, palpating for vitals. He assessed the context of the scene and said something to his partner, who was conducting her own evaluation of Margo. He swiftly reached into his bag, came up with a Luer lock syringe. He stabbed it into Jolie the Former's left thigh, and as the naloxone surged through her body, so did a firestorm of perception that Jolie the Visitor could feel: every notion of pain and sadness she had ever known all rolled into one.

She was transported yet again, this time to a place that was wholly dark save for a sliver of light from above. A distant plea rained down, and Jolie knew that she had to find a way out before the Toybox got any more clever ideas. Blindly, she began to claw through a welter of matter, wet and slick, gripless. She slid over the moist surface, inching toward the light, making pitiful, wounded sounds in her mind.

It's an illusion, she thought. *It's a game. It can't really hurt you.*

But it *was* hurting her. Laying her hauntings bare, assaulting her with unrepentant cruelty. It exposed her guilt, her regret, the psychological scar tissue that had healed but would never be the same as it was before the damage. She slithered onward through the mess. The splinter of brightness became a ring as she neared it, not large, but bigger than it had been a moment before. As soon as she was close enough to reach for it, she shoved her hands through the opening and pried with everything she had. It gave, slowly, and she pulled herself through the narrow crevice, spilled into the light.

Jolie the Visitor wiped out on firm flooring, and it was with a new horror that she turned to find her carbon copy still on the ground as it had been before she was drawn into that realm of lightlessness. It defied explanation, but she had somehow emerged from her own mouth.

Before the paramedic, her former self, gray as ashes, opened its eyes in a rabid display, sat up like an entombed vampire, and drank a violent breath. The medicine had saved her from the clutches of death.

In another blink, she saw the room from her revived vantage point on the floor and realized that the Visitor and Former self had become one again. She turned her attention toward the paramedics. "Go help Margo!" she shouted. "Please!"

They didn't so much as flinch.

"Please go save her!" Jolie pleaded again.

But the paramedics simply evaporated.

"Oh God," Jolie cried. She scrambled over to her friend on the futon. Margo was bloodless and still, a pink-tinged fluid pooling between her lips. Jolie put her head to the girl's chest and heard no evidence of a heartbeat. She started chest compressions, something she hadn't gotten to do the first time, and counted off as the tightness of Margo's ribcage resisted. Jolie was well aware that her efforts weren't working, but she continued anyway.

Then, when hope was at its lowest, a twitch in Margo's face. Her trademark smile warped her lips and sent a dribble down her chin, but her eyes remained shut. Jolie paused, waiting for her friend to speak.

And the girl did: "Stay with me, Jolie," she said, words spraying flakes of bloody foam. "Stay with me always."

Jolie began to weep. She wanted to stay, felt like she deserved to. But beyond her distressful yearning, she knew the score. She knew that Margo was beyond physical salvation. She knew that the talking body next to her was the figment of a cruel imagination. Nothing more. She knew that this was all a trap. The Toybox wanted her as a plaything forever. It was time to escape.

Jolie kissed Margo on her cold cheek. She got her feet under her and broke for the door as the room collapsed on itself. She twisted the knob with both hands. The door didn't open. In the split second she had left, Jolie dug deep. She plumbed the most umbrous and hidden corners of her soul, screamed them to the surface, showed them to the daylight. She tried again.

Jolie broke through the water, disoriented and out of breath. Her limbs were as good as feathers, flailing about in the dark. How brutal it was to break free of one hell, only to turn up in another. That's what recovery had been to her: a harrowing road with no obvious destination. The only rule was that she just keep going. She had run like mad and prayed that she didn't get caught by whatever was chasing her.

She wasn't ready to give up yet.

Jolie summoned whatever strength she could find and pushed upward on the lid, squinting as her eyes adjusted to the light pouring in. She heaved herself out of the sensory deprivation chamber, took a spill on the floor. Water dripped from her skin and hair as she recovered her clothes and beelined for the door, done with this game.

The Toybox offered little in the way of resistance as Jolie left it behind without once looking back. She navigated through the woods, half-naked, bare feet on dead leaves, the air cutting her down like a chainsaw. The threat of hypothermia paled in comparison to what she had just endured. One symbol led to another until she was back at the blackboard tree, surrounded by its offensive stench. A creature that had no business here. Jolie started for the car, where she would re-dress herself and let warmth ache back into her bones.

Halfway across the road, the voice drifted in on the wings of a feeble, malodorous wind: "Jolie."

Jolie glanced back to the image of Margo at the flank of the blackboard tree, not as she had been at the hour of her death, but as she had been in life: fearless, supercilious, beautiful. The girl smiled and lifted her hand in a simple wave. Then she retreated behind the tree, and she didn't reappear.

Jolie tried to wave back, but she was too late.

She walked the rest of the way to her car and got in. Everything drew level with her there in the stillness of the cabin, and she cried. She cried with her entire body. She cried until the need dried up. In her mind, she had suffered, surely, but had she atoned? How could she? Maybe living was enough. Maybe asking more of herself wasn't fair. Maybe the streets of Heaven and the Earth were lined with broken people like her, and maybe, just maybe, they would be mended someday. Made whole by their own forgiveness.

Jolie got herself together and started the car. She headed back to the truck stop diner in Flat Rock to tell Bonnie about the scariest place she had ever been.

The Light on the Other Side
of the Crawl Space

There ain't a whole lot I can say with any degree of certainty, but I can promise you this: There's nothing scarier than a damn spider. People say they're more afraid of us than we are of them, but I doubt it. They say it don't make sense to have a conniption over something a thousandth your size, but I beg to differ.

Look at it this way: A fiddleback spider no bigger than a penny packs enough hemotoxin in its bite to make the skin on your bones melt away like the fat on a pork butt in a slow cooker. Those little bastards can survive up to five seasons in the dark without food, too. And imagine how hungry they are when they finally *do* eat.

How can you trust something like that?

Them sonsofbitches are always there, always lurking, always ready. There's never more than ten feet between you and the next one. Statistically speaking. When it comes down to it, they've been around for hundreds of millions of years longer than we have. They were here before us; they'll be here after us. We're just passing through their world.

Nothing scarier than a spider. Well, almost nothing. I learned that firsthand in the summer of 1987, when I was twelve years old.

My Uncle Cecil was a hard man to know. Some say it's because he got beat silly as a little boy. Some say it's because he worked at the DMV for twenty years. Some say it's because of all that creekwater moonshine he drank. Whatever the reason, he was surly, and I honest-to-God can't remember a time when he was any different. Still, I was grateful that he took me in after his brother, my daddy, went to jail and my mama run off. I wasn't no more than four when that happened. And I didn't see the writing on the wall for a long time after that.

We lived in a haint blue vernacular house in rural Hickory, North Carolina, a place where your nearest neighbor was a quarter-mile away. One Saturday morning, about a year before what happened in the crawl space, we were all at the breakfast table eating biscuits and gravy. Aunt Glennie was poking at her food with a fork, never looking up, and my cousin Scott was leering at me like he always did when his daddy wasn't paying attention. Uncle Cecil was too busy shoveling slop into his mouth. He was tall and rail-thin, but he had a voracious appetite that didn't never seem to get sated. He was just fixing to lap his plate clean when something scuttled onto the front page of the newspaper beside him. A tiny spider.

I staved off a scream and spoke in more of a croak than a human voice: "Uncle Cecil. Spider."

He cut those wolfish eyes of his toward the *Daily Record* and licked sawmill gravy off his fingertips. Then he come down swift with his right hand, stunning the spider. It immediately rolled onto its back and folded its eight legs inward. Uncle Cecil returned to his breakfast without so much as a word.

"Cool," Scott said, his chair scraping the linoleum as he scooched away from the table. He took the paper in both hands. "Come here, Mina."

"Stop it, Scott," I shrieked, jumping out of my seat. I began to make for the living room.

Scott knew about my arachnophobia, and he loved to torment

me for it. He was always telling me about these documentaries he watched. Amazonian villages where the spiders ate chickens and the natives designed their huts specifically so that spiders wouldn't carry off their small children. One time at a mom-and-pop zoo in Coates, we saw a Goliath spider the size of a dinner plate. When I had tried to run away, Scott pushed me toward the cage.

"It's just a cellar spider," Scott said as I tried to round the couch. "Ain't even alive."

"Cut it out!"

"Come on, just a little pet."

About that time, Uncle Cecil cleared his throat and shot his son a look—and that was that. The man's stare was colder than an outhouse in the winter. Scott froze where he stood and frowned. Then he slowly walked the newspaper back over to the table and laid it there.

Aunt Glennie leaned in to take a closer look at the corpse. "Lord God," she said. "That ain't no cellar spider. That's a recluse."

"The hell you say," Uncle Cecil said dully.

"Lookit. It's shaped like a fiddle."

Uncle Cecil inspected it for himself. "Well, shit, how can you tell with it all smashed up like that?"

"I seen them before," she said.

"Glad I'm married to an expert," Uncle Cecil huffed.

"These is dangerous, Cecil. There's probably a mess of them under the house. Liable to poison us all. My brother got bit by one when we was little, and they almost had to lop off his pinky finger."

Uncle Cecil crossed his arms.

Aunt Glennie was skirting around the real issue, which was that all summer we'd been spotting more spiders inside than usual. They hung in the corners, they perched on the countertops, they blended in with the hardwoods. Most were everyday house spiders, a few were wolfs and granddaddy long-legses, but some were noticeably different.

Aunt Glennie collected the dishes from the table and walked them to the sink. "We got a spider problem," she said. "I just wish you'd fix it, is all."

"Well, I wish you'd shut the hell up," Uncle Cecil barked. He wiped his face with his napkin, cursed under his breath, and stormed through the screen door at the side of the kitchen. Off to his workshop, a converted barn house, where he tinkered on his lawnmower and other things.

Aunt Glennie stood at the sink for a long time, looking out the window there. She was going gray twenty years before her mama had.

"You okay, Aunt Glennie?" I asked.

"Yes, darling," she said.

"Why does Uncle Cecil spend so much of his time in that dark, old shed?" I asked.

"Some things don't belong in the light," she replied without looking back at me.

Uncle Cecil's meanness didn't stop at ugly words. I was maybe six when he come home the drunkest he's ever been. Or maybe it was just the drunkest I'd ever seen him. There was a time when Scott could've probably told you about it better than me. I remember it like a movie you keep on for background noise: some lines you recall, some you don't. Maybe I've just chose to block it out for the sake of my own sanity.

It was the middle of a Sunday, and Uncle Cecil had been out guzzling white lightning and shooting shit behind the Buffalo Lodge with his buddies. Gallivanting, as my Aunt Glennie called it. He staggered in the front door redder than a beetroot, his shirt tail half untucked, a sprig of hair dangling over one of his glassy eyes. Me and Scott turned away from the matinee movie on the television set. Aunt Glennie lifted her head from the wash she was folding on the couch.

"Fix me something to eat," Uncle Cecil said to her. No please, no nothing.

Aunt Glennie didn't bat an eye. "What would you like?"

"Fry me up a Treet sandwich," he slurred.

"All right," she said.

She walked into the kitchen, and he stumbled behind her. He

plopped down at the table. She grabbed the canned meat from the cabinet, fetched a frying pan. The silence that followed was so thick it clogged the room like a filthy wad of hair in a narrow pipe.

"Where was you at, Cecil?" Aunt Glennie asked. I think her back was turned to him.

"Out," he said.

"Preacher had a good message this morning. Mighta done you good to hear it."

"Don't give me your shit, woman," he hissed. "I had better things to do."

"Like Lucille?"

Years later, I'd hear through the grapevine that Uncle Cecil had run around with several women, but none more than Lucille Furr. That time in the kitchen was the first Aunt Glennie brought it up. And if I had to wager, I'd say it was the last, too.

The next part was and still is a blur:

Uncle Cecil hopped out of his chair. I can still hear the clang of that frying pan as it hit the floor. Aunt Glennie's yelp like a scared animal. I can picture Uncle Cecil bestride her, fingers wrapped around her face, mashing her head into the ground. Grunting and spitting and saying the godawfulest things. I hugged my Raggedy Anne and hid behind the other side of the wall as Aunt Glennie cried out in muffled bites of sound. Scott stood in the corner screaming, piss puddling at his feet. After a few minutes, Uncle Cecil pushed off of her. Then he heaved a guttural holler into the air and tore away toward his workshop.

And then there's the part I remember more than the others: Aunt Glennie laying there on the floor, sobbing. She was half shadow, half light there in the bare afternoon, her kicking legs searching for anything warm. Anything that would save her.

The day after the breakfast spider incident, I was in my bedroom getting ready for church. Aunt Glennie had laid out a pretty yellow dress for me, and I was standing there mid-clothes-change admiring it. Sometimes, I still feel like that youngin. Vulnerable and innocent. Light-begotten. But them days are long, long gone.

I brushed my hair behind my ears and reached for the dress, but something caught my eye before I touched it. A small brown hourglass with eight nimble legs sprawled atop the left shoulder. I breathed in, breathed out, forgetting my heart was there in my chest for a second. I was sure it was the same kind of spider as the day before. The little bastard skittered down to the waistline of the dress in the blink of an eye, and I jumped back and shrieked. That's when I heard the door creak behind me.

When I turned around, I saw Scott's wide, unblinking eyes there in the crack of the door. My cousin was an evil kid, and I mean that. He'd said all manner of vile things to me. But now he was staring at my exposed body. He was only two years older than I was, but he was the spitting image of his daddy.

I'd never felt so dirty or demeaned. I haven't since. I covered myself as best I could with my arms. Then I saw another set of eyes appear a head above Scott's.

"Boy!" a piercing voice called out, fracturing the quiet. "What in Christ alive do you think you're doing?" Uncle Cecil flung the door open, and there was a look of disgust on his face as his eyes locked onto me. A vein bulged on his forehead, and his lips quivered like he was a breath away from getting sick. He seized Scott by the wrist and yanked him wailing down the hall.

Moments later, I heard the screen door smack shut as Uncle Cecil dragged his son into the backyard, Scott yelling, "No, Daddy, no!" I threw on my overalls and raced toward those sounds of suffering.

Uncle Cecil had Scott by one arm under the apple tree, and with his free hand, he was beating my cousin below the short pants with a thick leather belt. He swung backward and forward indiscriminately like a tennis player as Scott danced and keened and begged, the dead fruits at his feet succumbed to the heat. "Damn you!" my uncle shouted.

"What in the world?" Aunt Glennie said, emerging from the back door. She processed the calamity in front of her for a second before she tried to intervene.

"Don't ever let me catch you looking at her cross again, you sinful little shit!" Uncle Cecil roared as he ribboned his son's flesh with blood-streaked welts. "Do you understand me?"

Scott didn't say whether he did or didn't.

Aunt Glennie wedged herself between the two. "Quit it, Cecil! You're gonna kill him."

A brief struggle ensued before Uncle Cecil come over the top with the belt and cracked Aunt Glennie across the face with it. She spilled to the ground, and he proceeded undeterred. Aunt Glennie crawled toward Uncle Cecil, hugged his ankle, screamed.

He jerked his leg upward and lashed her twice more. "Stay out of it!"

It went on like this for much longer than it should have 'til I stepped forward. "Take your goddamn hands off of her!" I hollered with a voice that seemed to come from somewhere else. Somewhere hidden underneath.

Uncle Cecil stopped and gave me a good look over. "What'd you say to me?" he asked, out of breath.

"I said take your hands off of her."

He stepped over Aunt Glennie, nearly tripping on her, and strode up to me. If only for a moment, it looked as though he'd turn the belt on me next. He licked his lips. "You better watch it, girlie," he said. "You'll turn into a filthy-mouthed whore bitch like your mother."

"Don't talk about my mama," I said. The tears were burning my eyes. I balled up my fists, and Uncle Cecil saw it.

"What're you gonna do?" he asked, pulling close enough to where he was towering over me. "You ain't got it in you."

I looked at my feet. He was right. I didn't have it in me. Not yet. When I raised my head again, he was disappearing into his workshop. A specter of a man in the overcast day slipping back into the abyss that had created him. A cursed place.

Under the apple tree, Aunt Glennie and Scott moaned and wallowed like people speaking in tongues at the churchhouse. It might sound nuts, but I couldn't tell if their cries were coming from their mouths or from the crawl space on the west side of the house.

Imagine this:

A little girl shows up on a doorstep, broken. Nothing but the clothes on her back. Stinking sweetly of methamphetamine smoke and dog piss. She's never been close with her aunt, has never known much about her, but Bitiah didn't know nothing about Moses when she drew him out of that river, now did she? The aunt, who has always wanted a daughter, cleans up the child and becomes more of a mother than the girl's own. Not outwardly affectionate so much as of inner strength and compassion. Teaches her how to read, how to tie her shoes, how to navigate the world as a child of God.

That was the story of Aunt Glennie and me. Both of us bonded over the hand we were dealt, the hard luck of life. Some might say she had a choice in the matter, but they'd be ignoring the whole story. Aunt Glennie suffered for the good of those around her, regardless of whether or not it should have been that way, and nobody knew that better than me. No matter how little I'd done to deserve it, her affection was unconditional. But she knew how hard the world was, especially for a girl, and so she didn't show me no more love than she thought was good for me.

There was this one time I came home from school upset because the other kids wouldn't let me play baseball at recess. I grew up a tomboy of sorts, my roughness and manner of speech taken from my Uncle Cecil and cousin Scott, and I could hold my own when it came to playing in the mud. But the boys didn't want to let a girl in on their game, and so I was cast out whenever I tried to join.

Aunt Glennie, straight-faced as an undertaker, said to me, "Just tell them boys only reason they won't let you play is they're scared of getting beat by a girl. That'll eat 'em up to so they can hardly stand it. They'll do anything they can to tell a gal she cain't do what she puts her mind to. That ain't true. You can. But you cain't just sit back and wait for it. You gotta have the will."

Next day, I did as Aunt Glennie told me. They pitched me the ball, and I put it over their heads. And when I told her what happened, all she did was nod. But I just knew she was smiling the next time I wasn't looking.

Most of the kids my age loved the summer because it meant no school. Not me. I wished I was anywhere other than where I was. I wished it for Aunt Glennie, too. A day after her and Scott got beat like dogs, I sat for hours in the dirt by the crawl space. The lattice-work stitched crisscrossed prisms of light onto the ground underneath the house. But after the first few feet, there was nothing. Or everything, for all I knew. It was a place of unimaginable mystery to me. Like the ocean or a cavern. Maybe there weren't spiders there. Probably, there were. I imagined slithering into that two-by-four chute toward the darkness. Wondered if there was enough magic in the world for me to come out on the other end into someplace that wasn't here.

The driveway was long, so I could hear Uncle Cecil's Buick approaching for a good while before he pulled up under the oak tree at the front of the house. He killed the engine, slung the door open, and moseyed up to the house with a Sunday stroller's gait. Then he went inside. Several moments later, he come out the back door, put his hands on his hips, and whipped his head around. Left to right, then back again. When that didn't quite satisfy him, he walked up to me.

"You seen your auntie?" he asked.

"No, sir," I said. Come to think of it, I hadn't seen Scott, either. He hadn't so much as blinked my way since the events of the day before. If I had to guess, I'd say he was sitting by the crick in the woods out yonder. There's one thing I do know for sure, though: He wasn't there for what happened next.

The engine of Uncle Cecil's Buick fired up to our left. We both looked off to find Aunt Glennie standing at the base of the oak tree. She was tying a length of rope around the trunk. Taking her time.

"What the hell?" Uncle Cecil mumbled.

As soon as Aunt Glennie had it fastened tight, she turned around. It was then that I realized the other end of the rope was knotted around her neck. A heaviness I'd never felt climbed into my throat as she settled into the driver's seat and slammed the door shut. Well, as shut as it would go with a rope lodged in it.

"Hey!" Uncle Cecil hollered. "What're you doing?" He took off in a brisk walk that soon became a sprint.

Aunt Glennie gripped the wheel. She turned her head, stared me straight in the eyes. She mouthed, "I'm sorry," blew me a kiss. Then she floored it, the tires spraying thatches of grass into the air behind her. The car went barking a stone's throw across the lawn and then bounding into a ditch at the edge of the property. The rope ran out of slack; it tightened straight. There was a horrific snapping sound, and Aunt Glennie's severed head went through the driver side window and thudded into the front yard. It bounced and rolled end over end for a good twenty feet before it landed right-side-up toward the road.

Uncle Cecil stopped dead in his tracks and stood still for a handful of engine ticks, smoke rising from under the hood of the Buick. He walked, snail slow and stupefied, to where her head lay. He picked it up, and the land became a quiet place where nothing made sense. What followed started out soft but became resounding, shattering the atmosphere in no time flat. Isolated, then everywhere. Like an airplane that's on the horizon, then the next thing you know it's directly overhead. Uncle Cecil howled, and his hysterics were so extreme that I couldn't tell if he was laughing or eat up with grief.

Scott come hauling ass from somewhere behind me. Uncle Cecil continued to cradle that head, to pet it. The world went colorless, and I threw up on my bare feet.

After the graveside service, where condolences were exchanged and "What a Friend We Have in Jesus" was sung, Uncle Cecil vanished into his workshop, and he didn't so much as poke his head out the door for three days straight. He spent mornings and afternoons glutting beers, and when the sun went down, he drank liquor out of a gas station soda cup. I went to check on him one morning only to find him passed out on the ground, belly-up with his shirt off. But to tell you the truth, I didn't care if he lived or died. He'd drawn the blinds on the one ray of sunshine I had left in my life. In my mind, even the slowest of deaths was too good for that bastard.

Once his bereavement pay was up, Uncle Cecil returned to work. But that's about all he did. He bought groceries but didn't put them away or cook. Us kids had to do our own laundry, pack our own lunches when school started back up. Fall came to pass. Then winter. There was no Thanksgiving or Christmas, but there *were* more spiders. A web in the doorway here, an egg sac there. If I saw one by itself, I smooshed it. If there were a couple, I bleached them out. Watched them curl helplessly 'til I felt empty inside.

Uncle Cecil didn't say a word to either me or Scott one way or the other, which was just fine by me, but sometimes I'd hear Aunt Glennie's name coming from the workshop at all hours of the night. Lamentations cast into space. The hootie owls were the only ones to answer.

Then one night in early spring, I heard something else. I thought it was just my mind playing tricks on me at first, but there was nothing illusory about the cries I heard as I laid in bed. These weren't from some dungeon of misery out back. They were in the house with me. In the cracks, the crevices, the darkest corners. I blinked myself awake, threw the covers back, and hurried to the room across from mine. I flipped the light on.

Uncle Cecil was straddling Scott with his hands around his son's neck, strangling him, lifting him up by the throat, and then slamming him back down on the bed again. "No!" my uncle yelled. "No!"

Scott gagged, face blanched underneath his father with wild eyes. He was digging his fingernails into Uncle Cecil's hands, but there was no breaking that death grip.

"I don't wanna do this, Glenda!" my uncle hollered. "Don't make me do this!" There was an otherworldly madness in his thousand-yard stare. Raw fear in his voice.

"Uncle Cecil, stop!" I shouted.

"You sick bitch!" he said to Scott.

"Stop!" I repeated.

"I'm gonna do it, Glennie! I'm gonna do it!"

"Help!" Scott wheezed, his face turning blue.

I closed my eyes and screamed so hard I felt a sharp pain in my throat: "Stop it, you evil sonofabitch!"

Uncle Cecil's body relaxed, and his eyelids flitted. He panted like he'd just finished a marathon, and he was drenched in sweat. Once he realized what was what, he turned Scott loose, put his hands on his knees, and stumbled back a few steps. Scott rolled off the bed and onto the floor. He scooted to the far corner of the room on his backside, gasping for air, clenching the fresh bruises on the skin of his neck.

Uncle Cecil gulped. "Oh, son," he said. "It was horrible. Your mama—" He broke down in tears. It was the first time either of us had ever seen him do that. "Your mama was a spider."

My uncle paused like he expected Scott to say something, but he didn't. Neither of us did. We just stared at him.

"A goddamn spider!" Uncle Cecil roared. "Her head had eight eyes, and she was carrying it in her legs. There was—there was slobber and pus running down her fangs and across her body like fucking fiddle strings." He tried to convey this with gestures as a mixture of tears and sweat dripped from his nose onto the hardwoods. He refused to make eye contact.

All I could think about was Aunt Glennie's head skipping through the grass. Her decapitated body still slouched behind the wheel, thin streaks of red leaking down her neck like spider legs. Her soul floating away on a stray breeze like a strand of web broke off from a tree. Its destination unknowable.

"It wasn't nothing but a fever dream," Uncle Cecil assured himself. If I didn't know no better, I'd say something like a laugh escaped him. "That's all. Just a shittinass fever dream." He exhaled. "I'm losing my mind," he said. He collapsed to the floor, and if there was an end to the tears, I didn't stick around for it.

Eventually, Uncle Cecil started calling in to work sick multiple times a week. Then by the summer of 1987, a few months shy of a year after Aunt Glennie's suicide, he stopped going at all. He grew a long, lacy beard, and his already-gangly frame withered to bone. The morning after the first big thunderboomer of the season, I walked into the kitchen to find him sitting at the breakfast table with a glass of milk, looking at nothing in particular, hands interlaced in front of him. He was wearing one of Aunt Glennie's dresses. Iris-blue. I still don't know why I done it, but I pulled up a chair next to him.

We must've sat there in silence for fifteen minutes. At one point, I waved my hand in front of his face, but it didn't break his trance. That milk stayed at the same level in the glass, the film at the top bubbling in the humidity. Suddenly, Uncle Cecil got up without a word. Like a voice I couldn't hear was calling him. He exited the back door, and I went to the window above the sink to see what he was up to.

Uncle Cecil was ducking by the side of the house in that dress, which barely went past his groin. He looked like something out of a sketch comedy program. In one effortless motion, he removed the latticework of the crawl space and chucked it behind him. He briefly peered inside, dropped to the flat of his belly, and slinked under the house. "Just call the Orkin man," Aunt Glennie had said so many times before. But he was stubborn. I reckon he wanted to take matters into his own hands. I reckon her voice finally got through to him.

As soon as his shoes disappeared into the crawl space, I zipped into Scott's room. My cousin was sitting on his bed with the lights off, eyeballing and fingering something with intense focus. It wasn't 'til I got closer that I realized he was picking the legs off a spider, one by one.

"Scott," I said. I could feel myself cringing.

He didn't divert his attention.

"Scott."

"Go away," he said, disinterested.

"Scott, we need to get some help. Your daddy. He's gone up under the house. I think he's finally gone off the deep end."

He plucked a leg. "What do you care?" he responded. "This is all your fault, you dirty skeeze."

I didn't even have time to think of what I wanted to say to that before I heard a shuffling below the floorboards. It was immediately followed by a thump. Then there was a scream, loud and continuous, that was so gut-wrenching it scraped my insides like an ice cream scooper against an empty carton. Scott finally looked up from his victim as that blood-cooling sound carried through the house uninterrupted for maybe ten seconds. When it ended, it was replaced by more frantic thuds and a squeaking I couldn't quite pin down.

Me and Scott rushed to the sink window. Uncle Cecil wriggled out of the crawl space and scrambled to his feet. He was swatting at his arms, legs, and torso. Smacking the back of his neck. Throwing punches at an invisible assailant. He inspected himself to his heart's content, raked his fingers through his beard. Once he'd seen all he needed to see—or hadn't seen all he needed to see—he lumbered across the grass of the backyard, which was now waist-high for the lack of upkeep.

Scott squinted. "Is he...wearing a dress?" he asked.

I ignored the question. I couldn't see real good, but it looked to me like Uncle Cecil was eat up with something. Riddled with red dots from head to toe.

The next day, I worked up the courage to go out to the workshop. It was a gorgeous day, but that didn't have the same effect on me as it once did. By that point, I'd learned that monsters were just as likely to lurk in the broad daylight as they were in the dark.

I passed beneath the tree where Scott and Aunt Glennie had been flogged so mercilessly. There must've been a dozen or so apples scattered about the roots. Kind of like my aunt and cousin had been that day. The fruits looked brown and rotten, writhing in the undulating heat wave. Upon closer inspection, I realized it was because an army of spiders had swarmed most of them, and now they were feasting, squirming, one inseparable from the next, like television static. The same squeaking I had heard under the floorboards the day before.

I recoiled out of instinct, brushing myself off to make sure none had got on me. Once I confirmed that I was free and clear, I continued ahead. The door to the workshop was half-open, and I had to coach myself up to come near it. I eased forward until I found myself on the threshold. The majority of the things inside were cloaked in shadow, but the morning sun seeped through in such a way that it cast a faint spotlight on the back of the room. What I saw there was unfathomable.

Uncle Cecil leaned back against his workbench, his silhouette gleaming with a pale, viscous discharge. His flesh—what was left of it—had erupted in scores of ragged, black lesions. The surrounding skin was gangrenous, sloughing away without much of a fight. To this day, I couldn't swear on it, but it appeared as though Uncle Cecil's body had morphed into the shape of a violin. Or at least it was well on its way. His abdomen bristled with fine short hairs. Only one of his arms looked mostly the same. The other was becoming narrow, segmented, angular.

A whisper came, and I jumped so hard I didn't think my skin would hold me. "Huh?" I said.

"Come in here, Mina. With us." It was a soothing voice. The voice I'd been looking for in a father figure my whole life.

"No," I said.

Uncle Cecil rocked forward into the light. Two dyads of drooping black eyes dressed the side of his face that I could see. "Come on, girlie," he said. "You'll never know if you don't try it. What do you say?"

I backpedaled one step, two. Two more. Then I tore off toward the house and left that bastard to rot in his sins. I made up my mind, and it was long overdue: I was getting out of there.

I got some belongings from my room and shoved them into my backpack with no regard for neatness. I didn't know exactly where the police station was, but I reckoned I could find my way into the neighborhood. I hadn't gone before because, to most people, Uncle Cecil was a decent man who was merely afflicted with a hot temper. I was just an imaginative little girl. But once they got a load of him now, no one would be able to deny what he'd become.

I went to Scott's room, where he was doodling black holes into a composition book. They reminded me of the eyes I'd seen in the workshop. "Last chance, Scott," I said. "I'm leaving."

He chuckled. "Where do you think you're gonna go?"

"Away from here."

He kept on scribbling. "To Hell with you, then," he said. "We don't need you."

I wanted to feel sorry for him, but I couldn't. It used to be awful hard for me to not see the good in someone, but in that final moment, all I saw in my cousin was his father. That mean-heartedness hatching and spreading, a cellar-like soul infested with maliciousness. A place where hope didn't exist.

"All right," I said. "So long." I began to turn away when that shuffling sound beneath the floorboards filled the house again. It dragged on, so unpleasant I could feel it in my teeth. Like someone sanding a piece of wood. It grew louder, drew closer. Only after it had settled directly below us did the restlessness cease.

Scott slipped past me in the doorway, made his way outside. I trailed him, clutching my backpack straps. We rounded the house through the overgrown grass. The opening to the crawl space seemed to yawn at us with its black obscurity. A two-by-four window of an unpredictable shadow world. Scott tiptoed toward it, but I stayed back. My cousin knelt down next to the entrance.

"Daddy?" Scott said.

There was one squeak. There were a million squeaks. Had I willed them?

A pulpy arm, overrun with fiddleback spiders, shot out of the darkness and latched onto my cousin's ankle. Scott fell to the flat of his stomach, shrieking, and a wave of them darted up his back, dancing in movements of unholy, gluttonous joy. A carnival of starving little demons at a meat buffet. He clawed at the dirt and hollered at the top of his lungs. "Help!" he cried. He skidded halfway into the crawl space. "Help me! Help me, please!"

I didn't.

Blackness swallowed Scott up to his neck, and he vanished into that chamber of despair along with the arm. The spiders retreated back in there behind him. His words still echoed after he was gone, but I could no longer discern them. I stood there for another minute or two, waiting for that fleet of spiders to come get me. But they never did. I sat my bookbag in the grass. And what I did next, I'll never understand:

I went to the workshop, my body befallen with a weight that left me dead tired and a little funny in the head. Was there a smile? In the distance, Scott's screams flooded the countryside until they became the air I breathed. Uncle Cecil's did, too—his guilt spinning webs of grief in intricate patterns. I laid down in the sawdust next to the lawnmower—not quite content, but not quite numb, either—'til day become night and night become day again.

Then I walked out into the light.

riverkeeper

The banks along the Neuse are swollen and unsettled, and if you didn't know any better, you would swear that something has been freshly buried beneath them. A soul waiting to be reunited with its flesh on the last day. Begrimed water brims there in the Coastal Plains like soapsuds in a too-full bath, remains of the foulness that has been rinsed from the land. Coursing, breathing, all the way to the Pamlico Sound, recycling, and eventually, redeeming.

The locals say something changed in the water after Matthew, but the riverkeeper stays the same. Those whom you're not supposed to talk about at the dinner table—the heretics—kneel to him as he passes, a godhead presiding over the only place on Earth where the lightning bugs flash in synchrony. Damned stars cast among the living.

After the extraction, the riverkeeper cradles the head in his webbed fingers and dunks it into the black. And maybe when it emerges, it will rise anew. A child, a creature of the breaking night.

It had been an otherwise normal day for Elmore when the accident happened. He was driving his cable van home after a full slate of jobs, guzzling what had to have been his eighth or ninth soft drink of the day. Anything to keep him awake until he crossed the threshold of his front door. He spent what little time he had at red lights scrolling through his arsenal of dating apps and smacking his cheekbones.

"Wake up, peckerhead," he chided.

But it was no use. Elmore was tired all the time. Plumb wore out, even after a full night of sleep. It was the only thing about his life he would have changed. Until that afternoon. He skated through downtown Kinston on auto pilot, shifting his eyes every so often to admire his attractive, if not heavy-eyed face in the rearview mirror. Each glance found his eyelids lower and lower, the drone of the engine a lullaby, until consciousness left his body like a transient ghost. For the few seconds he was out, he saw a shape. Something geometric, serpentine, bobbing just beneath the surface of his sentience. Something Hell-begotten.

What Elmore didn't see was the pizza delivery car blow through the red light and crash into the back half of his van on the driver's side. He didn't see the ladder fly from his roof, an accidental projectile, striking and snapping the neck of an innocent bystander. He didn't see his van skid, then teeter on its two passenger-side tires like a doomed Jenga set before it rolled over. He only saw that loosely formed, ophidian being of his imagination, moving in never-ending question marks as a musty smell flooded his sinuses.

Elmore came back to the world as a man lifted him through the driver-side window. He was right woozy, but he had been in worse shape after a twelve-pack of beer.

"You all right, Mister?" the man asked.

Elmore didn't answer him. He cast his eyes to the crumpled sedan behind him, now absent its light-up roof topper. It was totaled. A handful of people surrounded it, crouching, craning, anything they could do to see inside. Another few congregated by something on the sidewalk—something that Elmore would later learn was the woman slain by his ladder.

"EMT's on its way," the man said. And then he made a remark to another person who had come over to check on the situation: "I think this feller's fucked up pretty good."

Elmore dabbed above his top lip with the tip of a finger. A substance the consistency of wet mud was trickling from his left nostril.

Someone is lonely tonight. Someone is lost, a watermelon-sized hole aching in their chest. They hear he can make it better. They hear, by starlight, he can conjure dreams into the air, wring sorrow out of the heart like water out of a washcloth. Make them whole again.

Come into me.

Or maybe something darker.

When Florence's outer bands drifted inland, the entire region was inundated. Coal ash circulated upstream, unavoidable and diffusible, like bad thoughts. Settling as sludge on the river bed. The riverkeeper remained the same, a watchful guardian, as the waters receded, meandered into the ocean, the ground. Life was a big-mouthed bass, lapping up the runoff. Time was impossible.

The heretics, defectors of this lamenting world, allow him to drink of them now. Drink of their nature, their pain, the things we cannot see.

The adrenaline wore off at the hospital, and that's how Elmore learned his airbag had not deployed. He had lunged forward onto his steering wheel, fracturing four of his ribs. He had cut his forehead on his sun visor, burned his skin with his seatbelt. He was busted up, but that was the least of his concerns. He had dozed off at the wheel, and there was no doubt in his mind that people had gotten hurt. Maybe worse. And there was a nagging truth beneath it all: Elmore didn't really care so much as long as he didn't get in trouble. Not yet.

A nurse who had given him a merciful dose of painkillers an hour earlier pulled back the curtain. "We're gonna discharge you soon, Mister Elmore," she started, "but there's someone who'd like to have a word with you first."

Elmore's stomach turned as a policeman, uncommonly young and fit for this neck of the woods, came into the room. "Mister Elmore," he said in a thick tongue. "I'm Officer Boyette."

"What's this about?" Elmore asked.

"As you may or may not know, we don't normally get involved in automobile accidents unless there's casualties."

"Casualties?"

"That's right," Boyette said, unmoved. "The driver of the other vehicle failed to reduce speed at the red light and t-boned you. He was declared DOA." He squinted over his little clipboard. "Witnesses confirmed the whole thing. It was about as clear-cut of an at-fault as it could be. But I still have to get a statement from you."

"Hold up a minute," Elmore said. "You said *casualties*. Plural."

Boyette looked at Elmore very matter-of-factly. "Well, unfortunately, a pedestrian did lose their life."

"How?"

"The ladder on your truck dismounted and struck them. Kindly a freak accident. They were DOA as well."

This was all so unsettling and incomprehensible for Elmore, an idea he could see but not touch. He adjusted himself, fidgeted with his hospital wristband. His mouth was dry. "Am I gonna be charged for that?" he asked.

Boyette paused. "No," he said. "Not yet, at least."

"Well, shit," Elmore said. "I was on my way to the house, been up since five-thirty this morning. I'm just minding my business, and next thing I know, I'm being pulled out by a stranger, my van's on its side, there's glass everywhere. I don't remember nothing. Guess he blindsided me."

That wasn't entirely untrue; he just didn't mention the part where he fell asleep at the wheel. He had that convenience now that he knew he wasn't to blame for the actual collision.

Boyette jotted it down on his clipboard, his tongue hanging out of the side of his mouth. "Anything else you wanna add?" he asked once he was finished.

"No, sir."

"All right, then," Boyette said. He sized up Elmore one last time. "Look, you didn't hear this from me, but I seen that blue-line bumper sticker on the back of your van. You seem like a good enough guy to me, so my piece of advice would be to lawyer up about the ladder thing."

"I appreciate it," Elmore replied.

"You bet," Boyette said. He nodded his head, and then he was gone.

Elmore laid back in the bed, stared at the ceiling. It was hard to breathe. The physical pain would subside in a few weeks, he was sure of that. Cuts would heal, broken bones would mend. It was the time spent in his head that he worried about.

That night a crest in the Neuse, though there is no storm. They dance barefoot along the floodplain, a ceremony. A sacrifice to something greater. A tendril of motion shivers across the water's face, breaks into a million tiles of midnight. This hasn't happened, not like this, since 1954.

A waterwalker among them. The riverkeeper's robes are sawgrass and needlerush. His skin is naked and mucoid. His tongue, of a netherworld.

He's the only one who can talk to it.

The river spills over the banks, but only a little. In the devil's hour, a scream.

Elmore phoned a lawyer first thing in the morning. The attorney, a sharp, no-bullshit woman, told him they wouldn't get him in a criminal case, but the company he worked for might end up facing a civil suit (on account of the improperly secured ladder and all). He tried to not worry about it, but he did. He doped himself with twice the prescribed dose of his pain medication and filled out some worker's comp papers his boss had emailed him.

Then he did something really stupid: He added a few beers into the equation. He wandered around his house from room to room, feeling weightless and flat, a song on the stereo. Feeling like he wanted a cigarette, though he had quit a decade or so ago, in his mid-twenties. But there were also sensations that weren't so easily assuaged, those he may have considered psychobabble bullshit at one point in time. Depression. Post-traumatic stress. Guilt. Elmore had never felt guilty about anything, but then again, none of his fuckups had ever cost anyone their life. This episode seemed hellbent on making up for lost time.

Elmore entertained the idea of a distraction. He thought about texting Jenni—a woman he used for sex, a woman who used him right back—but in his condition, he doubted he could perform. He even thought, if only for the briefest of moments, about the thing in the shoebox under the bed. He did that from time to time when left to his own devices. Eventually, he chose the last solution he should have chosen, and opted to go for a drive.

He roamed the countryside in his rental car for maybe half an hour or so, veering off the side of the road several times and trying to fight off the urge to pick up a pack of smokes. There had to be some other answer out there in the dusk, and he thought he might have found it when he happened upon a dark structure in yellow silhouette a mile off the highway. The churchhouse was a beacon of radiance in that light-less farmland. Its sign—one of those boards with changeable letters—promoted Wednesday night service at 7:30. Elmore checked his phone. It was now 8:02 on Wednesday night.

"You know better," he said to himself as he pulled slantways into a space in the parking lot. Elmore avoided church like the plague. When he was a child, he had so much faith in things he couldn't see. Jesus directed his moral compass. Now, with everything he had learned about science, he had gotten away from it. Seemed to him religion was nothing more than an insurance policy for the scared.

Elmore *was* scared, though. He was terrified of what crawled there just beneath the surface, and so he removed the key from the ignition and made for the door on watery legs. He found himself in the back of the sanctuary, a room with vaulted wood ceilings, beadboard walls, and warm, muted lighting. There were maybe a dozen people in attendance, all in the first two rows, and none of them acknowledged this new visitor. Nor did the preacher. He was an old man with shoulder-length, mouse-gray hair and a patchy beard that extended well down his neck. Elmore sank undetected into one of the back pews. And that was fine by him.

"But what can we take away from Paul's first letter to the Corinthians?" the preacher asked, pacing along the altar with the conviction and animation of his megachurch contemporaries. "People hop at the chance to quote 'love is patient, love is kind,' but I think there's something bigger in there.

"Chapter ten, verse thirteen says, 'There hath no temptation taken you but such as is common to man: but God is faithful, who will not suffer you to be tempted above that ye are able; but will with the temptation also make a way to escape, that ye may be able to bear it.' Translation? God will never put more on you than you can handle."

"Amen," someone responded.

The preacher continued: "I have people saying, 'Preacher, I'm afflicted; Preacher, I hate my job; Preacher, I have problems in the home. Preacher this, Preacher that.' Well, we all have burdens, amen?"

"Amen."

"But I know *my* God. And I know that, my troubles aside, he'll see me through 'til homecoming." The old man flashed an asymmetrical smile. "What a day that will be, friends."

"Hallelujah!"

"What a day that'll be by the river of life. I'll be reunited with all the saints come and gone. My mama and them. My brothers and sisters in Christ." The preacher dropped his head, his joyous expression shifting on a dime. "But I've got a heavy heart for them that cain't say the same. Friends, there's gonna be a homecoming one day. Will you be there?"

Silence stole the room like a thief in broad daylight. The preacher lingered at his post, hands on his hips, a spare-framed psychopomp to a place of unimaginable cruelty. Where agreeable-enough warmth had been before, there was now stifling heat. A fever-dream of judgment.

"There's a harsh reality we all must face: If you die unrepentant of your sin, then Hell will be your home. Hell," he repeated. "A place where you'll be stripped naked as the day you come into this world and shoulder to shoulder in a brimstone pit of screaming rapists, murderers, pedophiles, nonbelievers.

"Imps and demons dancing to the sound of your pleas to a God who cain't hear you no more. A fire that burns hotter than anything on this planet, melting your flesh off the bone, only for it to grow back and happen again. And as soon as you think there's reprieve, it happens again. And again. And again."

Elmore knew how ludicrous it all sounded, but the uncertainty from his boyhood located him once more. What if it *was* true? And what if he hadn't faired so well in the accident? Would he be down there in Hell at that moment, getting tortured forever and ever? He examined his skin, imagined it liquefying and dripping to the floor, all his faculties and senses in high gear. Puke sloshed and climbed up his gastrointestinal tract, but he swallowed it back down.

By the altar, the preacher was now glazed with a film of fluid that was too viscous to be sweat. He seemed cold, sickly, more piscine than human. "There's only one way to avoid the fate we all deserve," he said. "And that's to be warshed clean. Any questions?"

Elmore shot up from the back pew in such a panic that he tripped and fell hard to the ground. He crawled the rest of the way out of the building on his hands and knees, and when he got to the car, he peeled off in theatrics he had only seen in movies. Behind him, his tires threw up great clouds of dust that looked like smoke rising above a lake of fire.

It occupies the local lore, a controversy. A misshapen revelation borne of the unholy water, weaving through the river, into the sewers, back again. Consuming shad, herring, eel, dead birds, detritus, filth. It lies dormant from December to June, subsisting off fantasies of its new birth, its new skin, last year's scales shedding and descending to the riverbed like the sail of a sunken ship.

Something meditating in the Atlantic, wrathful as it is beautiful, a horrible secret that nature keeps to itself until it's too late. The river-keeper feels it in his backbone. Now, in the sticky evening, he parts the sedge with a look, wades into the mystery. The time nears.

Elmore woke up behind the wheel of his rental car, sore all over, his clothes plastered to his skin, his breath tasting of shit. He checked his watch. Eight minutes before noon. He was in the parking lot of a Hunny Bunny grocery store with no recollection of how he had gotten there. He rubbed the sleep out of his eyes, started the car, and drove the rest of the way to his house. The night before was still fresh on his mind, but he made the decision right then and there that he was going to act like it never happened. Or at least try.

When Elmore got home, he showered, brushed his teeth, threw on a fresher pair of clothes. He needed to run by the junkyard and see what he could salvage from his van before they obliterated it, but his day was otherwise free. If he wanted it to be. He lingered on the threshold of his bedroom door for a while, the shoebox within sight. How easy it would be. How fast.

Go away, nasty thoughts.

He decided, instead, to put something in his stomach other than pills and booze—a piece of toast—and then he headed out to the county line.

It was an obvious comparison, but Elmore was surprised at how much the junkyard reminded him of a cemetery. The lot was organized in meticulous rows. Some of the vehicles had been unlucky, taken before their time. Others were well past their expiration date and had been shown mercy at last. Elmore found his cable van upright in the corner, the back left quadrant cratered-in like the surface of the moon. All the windows were missing, save the windshield, and three of the tires were blown flat.

The only thing Elmore could do now was shake his head. He opened the double doors at the back and began transferring items to the trunk of his rental car, his ribs smarting something fierce. Cable wires, tools, personal effects. He had almost finished packing up anything that was worth retrieving when he heard something off the side. A few cars down, a middle-aged man was grunting and cussing, tugging at a great jumble of metal. Elmore realized he was trying to open the door of a mangled sedan. The front end was gnarled and compressed. Nearly unrecognizable.

When the man became wise to the fact that someone was watching him, he stepped away, out of breath. He looked like Elmore might look fifteen years in the future. "I reckon it's a lost cause," he said, almost as if he were waiting for Elmore to offer help.

"Yeah, that don't look too good," Elmore agreed.

"Oh, I won't supposed to make it outta this one," the man said. "But I did, goddammit. Barely a scratch on me." He ran his eyes along the length of both arms to demonstrate. Then he considered Elmore's van. "What about you? Was your wreck purdy nasty?"

"Coulda been worse," Elmore said. He didn't know this person well enough to share that two other people—people with their own bodies and lives and plans and loved ones—had stopped living as a result of his mishap. "I've known of people who haven't made it out as good."

"I'll drink to that, brother," the man replied. He drew a flask from the back pocket of his Dickies, took a pull, returned it. "Name's Marty," he said. He extended his hand, a firm grip. The white liquor was strong on his breath.

"Elmore."

"Can I ask you something, Elmore?"

"Sure."

Marty pinched the bill of his dirty ballcap. "Have you felt a little off since it happened?"

"How do you mean?"

"You know," Marty said. "A little *off*. Take me. I've just been kindly blah the last couple days. Like things ain't quite right. Down in the dumps. Survivor's guilt or some shit. Hell, I don't know, I'm not a shrink."

Elmore was terrible at talking about his feelings, but the last thirty-six hours had left him all out of sorts. "Off is as good a way to put it as any, I reckon," he conceded. "I cain't decide if I dodged a bullet or if one hit me right between the eyes and I'm just too dead to know it. I cain't decide if I should be grateful or scared or both."

"I know what you mean."

"Hell, I don't have much use for organized religion," Elmore said, laughing a nervous laugh, "but I was so shook up that I went to a Baptist church last night looking for answers."

"See, that's where you got it wrong," Marty said. "They cain't help you." He scanned the area to make sure no one was eavesdropping, lowered his voice: "But I might know someone that can."

"That so?"

Marty leaned in close. "Anybody asks me, I'll deny it, but I've heard tell of this feller with special...abilities."

Elmore was listening.

"Lives off the grid out by the Neuse. Puts on some kind of ritual. Baptisms there in the river. Tends to this...thing...there."

Elmore cringed a little, reflected on the night before. *There's only one way to avoid the fate we all deserve, and that's to be warshed clean.* "If last night showed me anything, it's that I don't need no baptism."

"Naw, this is different," Marty assured.

"I don't know. Sounds fishy. Sounds like black magic to me."

"Just old-fashioned healing, is all," Marty said. His face held an expression of shock that hadn't been there before. Like he had just seen his car for the first time since the accident and was coming to terms with how lucky he truly was.

"I cain't even swim," Elmore added. "The thought of the river alone scares me shitless."

"Well... I've always been told that what we fear the most either destroys us or it sets us free."

Elmore thought that was well-put enough, but who was this stranger to be giving him words of wisdom? He stood there in that necropolis of cars, sweating his sins out, thinking life was the strangest goddamn animal. A slithery thing, existing on the edge of our subconscious.

"Lemme see your phone," Marty said.

Elmore didn't know why, but he coughed it right up.

Marty entered his contact information. "I'm headed out there tonight. If I hear from you, all right. If I don't, good luck."

An old green truck creeps to a stop in front of Elmore's house, and he meets it out there. Marty is behind the wheel in the same clothes from earlier, listening to a Classic Rock station, smoking a full-flavored cigarette that's almost down to the filter. "Hop on in," he says, like he has known Elmore his entire life.

Elmore does. The moon now ripe in the sky, an aqueous yellow cast as the two men wind through the backroads. If anything else besides crickets and other night things inhabits this plane of existence, it's a mystery to them. It's surreal to Elmore that he's here with someone he's just met, but he feels like he can't change it. Over the last several hours, he has thought about backing out. But a force has drawn him in. Something helicoid, constricting, addictive.

These are weird hours.

The drive is just shy of forty-five minutes, though in which direction Elmore can't say for sure. They pull off the side of the road in a stretch of nowhere, and for the first time, Elmore considers that Marty might have brought him out here to rob and murder him. But he doesn't really believe it. The pair exits the truck, enters a humidity that chews at them with wet teeth.

"What now?" Elmore asks.

"We're supposed to follow the light," Marty says.

"What light?" Elmore questions. Then he sees it, faintly pulsing somewhere behind the trees. There one moment, gone the next, back again.

"That one," Marty says.

Elmore nods.

The walk is another ten minutes or so into the woods, the throbbing light growing in clarity all the while. It's a rich greenish-gold that sends Elmore deep into his own head. He thinks about his life, crowded like the limbs of these pines. Some of it hidden, some of it in plain sight, like the roots below. Was it really that good before the accident? Had it always been leading him here without his knowledge? It is all so impossible to know.

An indistinct harmony spreads thinly through the undergrowth, even and consistent, a plainchant of restrained emotions that is decidedly part human. The other half is less identifiable. The volume rises. Marty pushes a lazy tree branch aside, and Elmore follows him into a clearing. He's rendered slack-jawed by what he sees there in the expanse before him. Hundreds of lightning bugs string the air like galactic clusters in space, a perfect timing to their bioluminescence. Dozens of hooded figures stand scattered in silhouette amongst the insects, and beyond them, the Neuse River sparkles starfire.

The monophonic song carries high into the night on the wings of foreign tongues. Above a commune. A holy place.

"Jesus, Mary, and Joseph," Marty gasps, removing his hat. "Ain't it beautiful?"

Elmore agrees that there's something enchanting about the scene, but he's not ready to commit to it yet. This is an event the likes of which he's never experienced before, a page out of a fantasy he hasn't even read. He's still trying to wrap his head around it—the bulblike lightning

bugs, the ceremonial music, the plutonian river—when two of the hooded shapes break away from the rest. They wear spectral auras, waft-
ing rather than walking, and smell of the hinterland after a good rain,
their half-human fingers spreading upward as if in kinship.

They're close when Marty throws himself into their arms. "Save
me!" he hollers, a throaty, desperate, drawn-out sound. "Save me! Save
me!" Within moments, a man who has been relatively tame and lucid
is reduced to emotional rubble.

The chanting grows louder still as the duo take him away, toward
the others, the lightning bugs, the riverbank. Elmore's adrenaline is in
the red zone of the tachometer, but he follows ever-so-cautiously. Marty's
cries fold into the other voices, and the flashing insects hover higher
into the sky. The other hooded figures part into two walls like the Red
Sea for Moses. And there, at the end of the channel, someone waits
knee-deep in the water. Him. The man with special abilities. The healer.
The riverkeeper.

Marty nearly collapses at the sight of him, and any remarks that
Elmore might have are left lodged in his throat. Scratching, irritating,
like a pin bone. The riverkeeper gestures for Marty to join him at the
edge of the bend, vapor ascending, silence falling. Marty lunges at the
riverkeeper's feet and clutches his robes, sends splashes jumping from the
water. He says something that Elmore can't make out, and with everything unfolding before him, Elmore is late to notice that the others in
attendance are surrounding them, closing in.

Background incantations ballooning in hallucinatory shapes. The
riverkeeper comes level with Marty, eye to eye, breaching his personal
space, close, in an animal way. Sizing him up as the scene becomes more
and more dreamlike for Elmore. The riverkeeper takes Marty by the neck,
gently, grants him a thorough lookover for a moment in which time
seems suspended. For some reason, Elmore surmises that the healer does
not approve of what he sees.

The chanting ceases.

And then, without warning, the riverkeeper clamps down with his
webbed fingers, crushing Marty's cervical spine. The sound is wet and

heavy, and it comes before the victim even has a chance to cry out.

Elmore screams fuck, or maybe he just imagines it.

The riverkeeper gingerly submerges the lifeless body into the murky water, drowning it, overkill, and before Elmore even knows it, he finds himself running. He goes no further than a few steps in the opposite direction before a mob of bodies swarms him. Elmore claws and rips and dead weights, all to no avail. He's being dragged backward toward the river, carrying on like someone in the throes of a night terror, the lightning bugs blinking, the treeline diminishing. Coldness seeps into the soles of his shoes, and then he's ankle-deep, shin-deep, kicking sweeps of water onto the bank. He feels something clammy on his shoulders and realizes that the riverkeeper has him, turning him inward, a visage of ghostly nothing under the hood.

The disciples retreat back to land, locking arms in a parabolic formation. The chanting resumes, more rhapsodic than before. Elmore seals his eyes as shut as he can get them. Maybe if he doesn't look, he won't suffer the same fate. Maybe he will wake up behind the wheel of his van, and this will all have been a dream. Perhaps his whole life will have been a dream.

Colors of fear present on the inside of Elmore's eyelids, pry them open against his will. A taste of dankness. The riverkeeper stares emptily into Elmore's face, as he had with Marty, holding him beneath the jawline with one slimy hand. With the other hand, the riverkeeper slowly peels back his hood. Translucent eyes bulge from the sides of a broad, moss-colored face. The riverkeeper's sheeny cheeks are studded with whiskered organs and moles of blood, his flat mouth yawning unthinkably wide.

Elmore turns away from the horror, but what he finds on the riverbank is no more comforting or believable. The disciples, the heretics, also begin to remove their hoods in succession. Most of them are unfamiliar, but Elmore recognizes a few. The cop is there, Boyette. Chants pour past his square jaw, become inseparable from the rest. The casualties of Elmore's crash are present, too. The innocent bystander, her head laying perfectly sideways on her shoulder. The pizza delivery driver, face caved-in, right eyeball dangling from its socket.

All of them are entranced. They've come back. They've come back for him.

Elmore faces the riverkeeper once again. He opens his mouth to scream, but nothing comes out. The riverkeeper plunges deep into Elmore's soul, treading, swimming there with those glistening eyes. He cups Elmore's head in his webbed hands, suggesting physical harm, but he doesn't break his neck.

No. He drinks of him. He inhales his inner contents like a sucker-mouth bottom-feeder on the floor of the river. Elmore can see them leaving from inside him like nets of bursting dreams, fireworks, the things he never knew were there. Coming and going, easy. The way water does. This is the extraction.

Once the deed is done, or nearly done, the riverkeeper eases Elmore into the water. This is the baptism. What lies beneath the surface is completely different from what Elmore expects: stonewort and hydrilla shine across the ever-deepening river floor like the streetlights of an underwater city. Everything breathes down here. A silty gray substance swirls in fine clouds as far as the eye can see, smelling of sulfur, and then, in the distance, an object bides in space. Barely perceptible. Waiting to be summoned.

Elmore feels the riverkeeper release him, but he can't move. He drifts further underwater toward the object on this strange city's outer rim. In a flash, the thing ahead is on the move, and in no time at all, it is rushing him. As it breaks into the light, Elmore sees that it is a monster: a head crowned with a trident of horns, elliptical eyes on a skull face, enraged. Its snakelike body, perhaps the length of three school buses, whips behind it as it closes in. Its mouth unfurls a thousand quills of teeth, and Elmore yells bubbles through the water. The river monster swallows Elmore, who zips down a gummy shaft like he's falling through a tunnel. He shatters through a stringy wall on the other end, enveloped in a fragile dermis that carries him back toward shallow water. The river monster wheels around, retreats to its biding place.

Invigorated, Elmore tears through the water, the sheath of skin.

Something has changed, and he's running. He's running, and nobody is trying to stop him.

Elmore retraces his steps through the stretch of flat land and the trees beyond it, anything and everything sticking to the coat of ooze his skin and clothes have spawned. Leaves and pine needles and spider webs. By moonlight, he sees the truck he arrived in, and he prays that by some miracle Marty has left the keys in the ignition.

No such luck.

Elmore opens the door, removes the cover on the steering column, and gets to work on one of the only things his stepfather ever showed him how to do: hotwiring a car. He tugs the right bundle aside, twists the correct wires together, breaks the steering lock, and speeds off down the road, checking the rearview mirror every few seconds. He doesn't know where he's going, but he doesn't care; it's away from here, and that's good enough for him.

The weight of the whole experience is damn-near suffocating. It's all Elmore can do to breathe like a normal person and not a fish out of water. He drives. He drives until he happens upon a filling station, and with the tank nearing E, he has no choice but to stop. When he enters the building, the frizzy-haired clerk stares at him like he's an apparition. Maybe he is.

"What in the holy hell happened to you?" she asks.

Elmore pulls out his sodden wallet, pitches a floppy ten on the counter. "Ten on number two, please," he says with a voice that's not his.

"Are you all right?"

"Ten on two!" Elmore squeals.

The clerk flinches. "Okay, okay," she says, keying it in.

"What's the fastest way back to Kinston?" he asks.

"You're on Forty-three. Turn left outta here, and you'll take that to Eleven South."

Elmore turns tail without saying thank you or sorry. Back at the truck, he removes the gas cap and inserts the pump without issue. But when he reaches to return the handle after he's done, the hose transforms into a sinuous creature, squirming and lashing on the asphalt below. Sprouting a head of horns with ill-intentioned eyes. Elmore shrieks and throws the pump to the ground, spilling the last of the gasoline. He nearly trips to get back in the truck, and races out of the parking lot.

There's a sensation of something behind Elmore's eyes, under his skin, trying to get out as Marty's Classic Rock plays in the background. He has a hard time focusing, accepting, fleshing things out in his mind.

What is he supposed to do? He can't go to the police on account of Boyette.

Who would believe him anyway?

How is he supposed to believe himself?

Then at least something of an idea comes to him. "I'll pack my shit," he says aloud. "I'll pack my shit and drive south 'til I cain't drive no more. Somewhere it cain't find me. Someplace without water. I'll bury this fuckery so far in the dust they'll need a plow to get at me."

The night stalks Elmore the rest of the way home. He rolls into his driveway in a truck that doesn't belong to him. He leaves the engine running. He stomps into the house, looking over his shoulder once, and heads for the bedroom closet. He snatches a suitcase from the top shelf. He has a mind to fill it up, too, but the sensation returns. Something *is* trying to get out. Or something is trying to get in. A blast of nausea shoots through Elmore's body. He turns, coughs a wad of something treacly to his left. Wet mud on the bedspread. Before he has a choice in the matter, he's on the floor.

The first thing Elmore sees when he awakens is the shoebox under the bed. It's staring at him as though it's trying to tell him something but doesn't know how. Morning light bleeds through the window, lean and unhurried, like blood from a papercut. A blink or two of the eyes passes before Elmore even realizes he's choking. He sits up, struggling for air, abandoning the plan from last night. Primal instincts have won out.

He turns violently onto his stomach, flip-flopping as he finds his feet. He digs at his throat, staggers to the hallway mirror. The last of his doubts evaporate there in the glass. His slick skin, now an ailing shade of sage, glistens like nail polish. A set of deep gills scores the flesh on either side of his neck, swelling, then shriveling, in dramatic gasps. Barbels bud from his cheeks in vinelike gestures, and his dilated eyes blacken into mindless wells. Elmore lifts his hands. Tissuey patches stretch there between the fingers.

He doesn't want to waste a thought while he can hold one.

He scrambles back to the bedroom and dives onto the floor. He grabs the shoebox and flips off its lid. Plugs the .45 into his mouth with both hands, tastes the steel.

It was always going to end this way.

But now it doesn't. A fury of miraculous power radiates from every pore across Elmore's body. He squeezes the grip of the gun, but not the trigger. He removes the barrel from his mouth, uncorking a deafening scream.

A deafening scream that only he can hear.

Elmore raises the gun above his head and spikes it to the floor. He takes off. He runs through the bedroom doorway while he still has legs, bursts through the front door of his house.

What we fear the most either destroys us or it sets us free.

Elmore doesn't know where he's going until he sees it. Down the street, seconds to spare, he launches himself into a storm drain. His changing form liquefies upon contact with the grate. Splashes into the road, the beading remains caught in the newborn rays of sun.

The riverkeeper tends the water, naked, alone. A prophecy:

It doesn't have a name yet. They never do at first. It was trapped in the warmth of an immense belly, and now it will rise upward, break through to the other side, and push toward higher ground. A hellmouth with fangs of thought.

It will change things forever.

It has been an underwhelming shell. Unsavory. Boring. Inconsequential. Carrying on good as dead, but maybe now it has a chance at life. Maybe it will be delivered from the water—he will be delivered from the water—shaped into something better, something that can shed its skin and swim clean through this unknowable existence, this place where everything flashes in synchrony—swells with light, then exhales the darkness that has always been there beneath the shallow.

False Awakenings

a bedtime story

Open up, goddamn you, Rae thought.

Not again.

Her eyelids were closed, but she could still see the room, moon-washed silver by the early morning hours. Her brain was awake; it had been for a whole minute now, going on two. Her muscles, not so much. She tried to will energy into them, but she was limper than a soggy, cold French fry from Fat Boy's down the street. This wasn't the bad part. Not yet, at least. It felt more like the end of a dream—the scary kind she'd had so many times that she could tell it wasn't real. But her condition was; this was already the second time this week that she couldn't move upon awakening, and it wasn't even Wednesday yet. She felt lucid enough until she remembered her limbs were inoperable. Then she realized that she was a prisoner inside of her own body again. A rolling current, warm and strange, surged through her chest and bubbled into her throat. And then the part that was always hardest for her to explain: the "presence." She had no logical reason to believe it, but whenever this happened, she always felt as though someone or something was lurking just beyond her bedroom door, which she now heard creaking slowly open.

Rae tried to scream but realized her mouth was closed. She could hear the muffling effect echo deep in her ears; it went back and forth with the churning waves outside. She wondered how long it would last this time. Five minutes? Ten? She'd never had an episode last longer than fifteen, or so she thought. But if tonight was a first, it would surely give whatever was on the other side of that door ample time to do what it came there to do. Suddenly, she sensed a twitch. Maybe a toe. She knew she was laying on her back, even though she had been urged to start sleeping on her belly. The "presence" felt close enough to breathe on her neck. Her entire body tingled. Then her leg moved.

"Rae." A whisper came, like air escaping from a balloon.

Her arms, encumbered by invisible kettlebells, rose gradually and lamely. And just as her throat began to tighten, she sprang up in bed and bayed like a coyote at the moon. Beads of sweat bloomed across her bare body as she glanced over at the door; it was as closed as it had been when she'd laid down hours before. She sighed and rolled over to the other side of the mattress. She buried her face into the pillow there; it still smelled like Clem's perfume, even after all these months—floral and strong, but not too sweet. Her girlfriend had always applied it so liberally. Oh, how Rae missed it.

She grabbed her phone from the nightstand and hit the green icon on the first number in her history.

It rang four times before a groggy voice answered on the other side. "What's wrong, darlin?"

"It happened again, Mama."

"Raeanne," the voice said, thinning out with consciousness. "Again?"

"Yep." She flipped on the bedside lamp. "But this time it was different."

Rae heard a rustle in the background, followed by a mumble from her mother. "Sorry, I was just letting your stepdad know everything's all right. Different, how?"

"It sounds foolish," Rae began, "but usually whatever I feel like is after me stays on the outside of the door, you know, just peeking in. This time, I heard it open."

"Hallucinations."

"I guess. It just felt so real."

"When do you go back to the doctor?"

"Next Monday."

"Make sure you tell her everything," she said in her most motherly tone. "I feel like you don't tell her everything."

"I will," Rae replied, sounding five years old again.

"Good."

"Mama?"

"Yes, baby?"

Rae sniffled. "When Daddy left, did you ever dream about him coming back?"

Her mother paused. "You already know the answer to that."

"It's just because, I thought this time it might be, you know—"

"Clem?"

She smeared a tear on her cheek. "Yeah."

"Clem's gone, baby," her mother said, the love in her voice tougher than rawhide. "She ain't coming back."

Rae nodded her head up and down as though her mother could see that she understood through the miles that separated them. "I love you, Mama."

"I love you, too, my Rae of sunshine."

Rae ended the call and swung her legs over the side of the bed. She grabbed an oversized t-shirt from the dresser and made up her mind to fetch a glass of water from the kitchen. On her way there, she was drawn to the sliding door on the back side of her house. She stood there, eyes on that pane of darkness for several minutes. She could hear the ocean, feel it, even though she couldn't see it. Rae reckoned a lot of things were like that.

"You've been sleeping in the supine position, haven't you?" was the first question she asked, and she hadn't even opened the door all the way before she asked it. Dr. Eloise Pender had been in med school when Neil Armstrong took mankind's first steps on the moon—she didn't have time to cut to anything but the chase.

"Yes, ma'am," Rae said, her legs swinging from the exam table.

Dr. Pender rolled one of the beads of her eyeglasses cord between her age-spotted fingers. "I thought we were trying prone," she said, smiling.

Rae was almost too ashamed to look at her. Instead, she focused on a collage made of sand dollars hanging on the opposite wall. "Well, it starts out that way, I think," she replied. "But then I have one of my episodes, and I realize I must've rolled over at some point."

Dr. Pender plopped down on her stool and scooted over to her computer. She squinted at the monitor and poked at the mouse. Then she picked it up and began to mash at the left clicker with her thumb. "I hate this damn thing," she said.

Rae suppressed a laugh.

"I must've treated a thousand patients with sleep problems over the years, Miss Raeanne." The doctor sniffed. "But I gotta tell you, you're a doozy if I ever saw one. From my experience, most people have fits falling asleep, not waking up from it."

Rae believed her. She had done the research. Less than ten percent of people reported experiencing similar symptoms at any point in their lives, let alone frequently.

"Let's see... We tried doxepin for the nightmares. No dice." She scrolled on. "Meditation-relaxation therapy. Might as well be pseudo-medicine," she mumbled. "You don't have narcolepsy. I don't suppose sending you back to Duke and having all those wires hooked up to you again would do any good."

Rae shook her head side-to-side, shuddering at the memory.

Dr. Pender sighed. "No, I just think you have a good, old-fashioned case of sleep paralysis."

"Sleep paralysis?"

Dr. Pender swiveled toward her. "It sounds more serious than it is. We call it 'false awakening.' It's more or less just a disruption in your REM cycle, but some patients chalk it up to supernatural phenomena—demons, incubuses, shadow people, night hags. There's literature on it from Scandinavia to North Africa to East Asia, and everywhere in between."

Rae pulled at the ring on her little finger. "I know it sounds crazy, but when it happens, I have this out-of-body experience, but I'm also locked inside of my body at the same time. I don't know where the hell I am, really. Excuse my language," she muttered. "But I feel like someone's there with me."

"Like something bad is there to get you?" Dr. Pender asked.

Rae nodded.

"They call that the Intruder."

"Oh. Well, of course you don't believe that." Rae blushed over a nervous smile.

"Demons? Not physical ones." The doctor rested her glasses on her chest. "But other kinds, sure."

Rae's face grew hot.

"I know you've had a hard time, child," Dr. Pender said, her gravelly voice flattening out. "It's never easy when someone who was in your life isn't there anymore."

Rae fanned her face. "I'm sorry," she said, trying to laugh it off.

"Don't apologize. If it's any consolation, sleep paralysis can't kill you."

"Well, it sure can make you wish you were dead," Rae said, dotting her eyes with the tips of her fingers.

Dr. Pender studied her. Then she reached for a prescription pad. "Why don't we try an SSRI for a few months and go from there?"

"Sure," Rae said.

Dr. Pender smiled. She rose slowly from her stool, patted Rae on the shoulder, and exited the room.

Rae glanced over at the mirror next to the door and barely recognized what she saw. She looked tired. Her once-round face now bent inward at the cheeks. Her eyes were budding feet, her skin waning, and even her hair seemed thinner—once a deep brown, now a fine, sandy color like the wet edge of a sound. Thirty hadn't been so unforgiving to her friends.

She trudged out into the hot morning, thick and briny compared to the conditioned air of the one doctor's office within a fifty-mile radius. She thought about dropping off her prescription at the pharmacy but reckoned she was late enough for work as it was. Besides, she had time later; she could make most trips here in ten minutes or less. Dallie Futch wasn't even a city or town; it was a census-designated place a crow's fly north of Topsail Beach on any map. The 6,000—give or take—who lived in this sleepy, salt-licked curve on the coast of North Carolina consisted mostly of retirees and beach bums who had come into a little bit of money. Rae was neither, but the area suited her just fine. She'd grown up an hour away in Wilmington, had gone to school there, and supposed this was the farthest inland she would ever make it—at least to live.

She drove two blocks and one right turn down Ocean Boulevard, her tires kicking up dusty clouds as she pulled into the parking lot of the Quarter Moon Café. She dragged past the arching juniper-wood trellis out front and into the local seller of knickknacks and bargain books. Mr. Socks, the resident cat, threw her a somewhat baleful glance before returning his head to the pillow he had fashioned with his paws. Rae tucked herself into a corner at the back next to a sign that read, "please don't pet the kit kit, he scratches," and unsheathed her laptop from her satchel. Then something dawned on her, wrapped itself around her like a winter coat. It wasn't a thought or a memory, or even an aura. It was a smell. For a split second, Rae knew it was Clem's perfume.

A thin, grizzled man emerged from the back of the shop and grinned. "Café au lait?" he asked.

"Please," Rae replied, shaking her head like she was coming out of a spell. The scent was gone.

She reluctantly opened her emails and found one from her boss. In a previous life, she had been a fiction writer, albeit not a particularly successful one. She had a drawer full of rejection letters to prove as much. Now, she wrote stories for the North Carolina Lottery in Raleigh. Whenever someone won $50,000 or more from a scratch-off, her boss faxed her a copy of their questionnaire, and she worked her magic to turn it into an interesting story for the company website. It wasn't much, but it allowed her to work remotely and paid her enough to scrape by at the beach.

The owner tabled her drink. "What's this'n about?" he asked.

"A waitress in the mountains won a quarter-million on the new ticket we put out last week."

His loamy eyes lit up. "Must be nice," he said, walking off and shaking his head.

Rae smiled. She looked ahead and cracked her knuckles. "Waitress, win," she whispered. "Win, Watauga." She pecked away at her keyboard, backspacing every few words. "Ticket serves up win for Watauga waitress," she said, and tabbed down. Her cursor blinked at her as she stared off into a rack of touristy t-shirts to her left. She withdrew her phone from her pocket and bypassed the lock screen. She opened her contacts and scrolled down, her finger hovering above the green icon next to Clem's name; she pressed it, but as soon as she did, she stabbed frantically at the adjacent red widget before she even heard a dial tone.

Fuck.

She didn't know how it had happened, but it had all the same: She was asleep. Rae could tell she had dozed off in the Quarter Moon because she was dreaming lucidly. How else would she be able to relive the events of what had happened on that day nearly five months before? They came to her not in their entirety, but rather as pulses and clips from a sinister highlight reel in a hellish, empty movie theater.

First, she saw rays of sun breaking across Clem's back as she offered her irresistible, sleepy smile. Then she watched Clem make love to her, fingertips running over naked skin like mid-morning wind on shallow water. Next, there was the overcast car ride to Wilmington, Clem belting out the lyrics to a random Spice Girls song along the way. Then it came, inevitable and devastating. Rae saw the two of them sitting there in the stands, Clem turned to her and grinning beneath her ballcap. The cracking sound passed swiftly, and the world fell to gray.

Rae's consciousness jolted into a new reality. She was firing on all cylinders in her mind, but her muscles and tendons and bones were immobile and numb. It didn't take long for her to realize the score: The thing Dr. Eloise Pender had called sleep paralysis had found her yet again. Panic reared its ugly head like an unwanted visitor, busting the lock on the door of her gut and letting itself in. Hyper-vigilance took over, and Rae could feel her heartbeat hammer through every bend of her screaming body. Through her mind's eye, she could see her surroundings— the shelves of books, the postcard racks, the coffee table with the starfish centerpiece. But something was amiss. A crushing weight blanketed her, but it couldn't be her MacBook. No, that was on her lap. This feeling settled heavily on her chest.

What had Dr. Pender called it?

The Intruder.

Rae mustered up enough willpower to peel an eyelid open, and though her vision was blurry and incomplete, she was horrified by what she saw. There, on her chest, sat a small goblinlike creature, the features of which were muzzy yet no less menacing. She couldn't make out much of it, only that it was about three feet tall and its skin was the dirty yellow color of bile. And the eyes—it didn't seem to have any. It crouched there, watchful and grotesque as if it were a gargoyle and Rae's chest its perch. It didn't seem to have any interest in moving.

Rae's other eyelid popped open, and suddenly a burst of electricity coursed through her upper body. She lunged forward in her chair and flung the creature to the floor, a banshee-like howl escaping her as she did so. She screamed twice more before the Quarter Moon's owner came running.

"What's the matter, Miss Rae?" he asked, eyes wide with alarm.

Rae white-knuckled the arms of her chair and looked at the floor to her right. She unloaded a heavy breath. It was Mr. Socks, and he looked rightfully offended. He shot her a deprecatory scowl before scurrying off to the front of the building.

"Miss Rae, are you all right?" the owner asked again. He crouched down next to her and waved his hand in front of her face. "What's got into you?"

She could feel the cold sweat cascading down her forehead. "I'm fine," she assured. "Just fell asleep and had a bad dream, that's all. A real, real bad dream."

The cat climbed into his bed near the store entrance.

Rae apologized for any pain she may have caused Mr. Socks, though the owner hadn't seen that part to begin with and told her not to worry about it. Then she packed her things and headed home. A sick day seemed like the right move to make after what she had experienced. Once she entered the house, she let everything in her hands drop to the floor, went into her room, and fell face-first onto her bed. She lay there for nearly ten minutes before she worked up the courage to get back up. She ambled over to the walk-in closet and opened the door. She flipped on the light, removed a shoebox from the corner of the top shelf, and unlidded it. The three-quarter-sleeve baseball shirt was wrinkled but not dirty. Except for the isolated stain of dried blood, of course. Rae studied it with weepy eyes. Then the gaps of the dream came flooding back.

Baseball was something that Rae and Clem bonded over, so when spring rolled around, they decided to attend the Saturday season opener for the Wilmington Longshoremen, the local double-A team. Rae stood in the kitchen in an old pink and purple leopard-spotted bathrobe she'd had since college—the one Clem teased her about religiously—fixing an omelet. She felt something sneak up on her and jumped a little bit.

Clem hugged her from behind and rested her head on Rae's shoulder. "You scare easy," she said.

Rae closed her eyes. "I knew it was you," she said. "Your perfume is a dead giveaway. I can smell you coming from a mile away, Clementine."

"You know I hate when you call me that."

Rae turned. "I don't know why. It's purdy," she said jokingly.

They kissed, and Rae went back to cooking as Clem stretched and gazed out at the beach.

"Jesus, it's almost one o'clock," Clem said. "We better get going if we're gonna get across the bridge and to the ballpark on time."

"Aye, aye," Rae responded with a goofy salute.

They left in Clem's car and put on a playlist of her favorite songs from the 90s. Chumbawamba, Meredith Brooks, No Doubt, and more poured through the speakers as Clem gripped the steering wheel and sang unapologetically in an off-key tone. Rae pretended to be bothered by it, but she wasn't. There wasn't much Clem could do that she wouldn't love. She was beautiful and ebullient in her matching navy blue Longshoremen hat and jersey, and Rae couldn't imagine a time she had woken up next to anyone else.

They arrived at the stadium with half an hour to spare, so they found their seats along the first-base line and bought a couple of beers. The brisk, gloomy afternoon began to sprout bands of sunlight as they goofed off while the players warmed up on the field. Clem adored this place, and it showed. The smells, the sounds, the ridiculous mascots. She was a fan of it all. Rae hadn't always seen Clem at peace, but she did anytime they were here.

The game was uneventful for the first four innings. Only one run scored, and it was in favor of the visiting team on an error. At the top of the fifth, a right-handed batter strolled to the plate and dug into the box. He watched the first pitch go by for a strike. That's when Rae nudged Clem, hoping to ask her if she wanted to grab another beer. Clem turned to Rae and beamed at her with those fiery green eyes.

A noise that sounded like a monster clicking its tongue filled the air.

Someone screamed, "Heads up!"

But it was too late.

There was another sound—this one somewhere between a chilling smack and a dull thud. Clem doubled over the seat in front of her. Then she sat up and palmed her head around the left temple, a rivulet of blood trickling from her nose onto her jersey. She had been struck by a foul ball.

An usher darted down from the concourse. "Are y'all okay?" he asked.

"No, she's not fucking okay," Rae hollered. She could feel the tears starting to come as she cradled Clem's head. Her girlfriend had quickly grown woozy and disoriented. She clasped onto Rae's arms weakly.

"We need a medic down here pronto," the usher called into his walkie.

An EMT carried Clem up the steps to the concourse and put her on a stretcher. Rae could feel every eye in the ballpark on them, but she didn't care. Clem didn't look good. She had lost a lot of her color, her face was starting to swell, and she didn't look like she knew where she was. Once they got outside of the stadium, Clem vomited twice—once before they loaded her into the ambulance and again on the way to the hospital.

Paramedics rushed her through the double doors of the trauma unit and left Rae sitting in the waiting room. She rocked back and forth, holding Clem's ballcap, the tears crashing in waves that seemed unending.

Back in the walk-in closet they had shared, Rae clutched the jersey. She held it to her face and disappeared into it. Then she crumbled onto the floor and wept, and she didn't get up for a long time.

After the operation to mend the acute intracranial hemorrhage had failed, Clem was on life support for three days. That's when her mother—who had been appointed power of attorney—stepped in and signed the DNR. Nobody blamed Rae, and Clem would have been the first person to admit that she should have been paying attention in the first place. But that didn't make it any easier. She had turned to look at Rae. Rae had distracted her. If she hadn't, Clem might still be there. And the culpability Rae felt for that was debilitating.

It was a freak accident, and Rae could relate. She'd had some pretty freakish things going on herself. A week had passed since she started taking the SSRI, and it wasn't making matters any better. Dr. Pender had said it could take as long as six weeks to kick in fully, but Rae wasn't hopeful and didn't know if she had that long anyway. She had experienced two more episodes in the last seven days alone, and both of them made her wonder if she would be better off dead. In the first one, the Intruder had merely poked its yellow head through the crack in the door and watched as Rae came to. During the second, it had crept halfway to her bed, a noise that sounded like a million fingernails drumming on Plexiglas preceding it, before she shot up in bed and screamed so loud she was sure that she would shatter her windows. Of course, the little demon was nowhere to be found either time.

After that, Rae surmised that she was running out of options, and so she did the only thing she could think of: avoid sleep altogether. She had been awake for a full two days when she decided to take a lunchtime trip out to the Dallie Futch swing bridge in the middle of the week. She parked her car on the lip of the road just before it and walked about halfway along the railing before she stopped. The bridge itself was a relic; it had been erected at the end of World War II, and it might have looked spiffy back then, but now it was green and rusty. It looked tired. Rae thought that was appropriate, given how exhausted she was herself. Her eyes were dry and full of sleepless fire, and her muscles felt like overdone oatmeal.

She stared into the water below. A gentle breeze had kicked ripples into the surface, which now eddied in carefree strokes. Rae decided it was well-rested, and she envied it. Sleep was the place where people and things found refuge, and if she couldn't say the same, what was the point? She knew that she couldn't stay awake forever. When that realization sank in, she squeezed the rails of the bridge and considered something horrible. And she might have gone through with it, too, had the wind not passed through when it did. A gust pushed her backward, only slightly, with clean, pungent notes of orange blossom. Rae removed her fingers from the railing and heaved a sigh, her head growing swimmy as she backpedaled away. She almost found herself in the middle of the bridge before she stopped. Then something told her to go back to her car, and she didn't offer any kind of rebuttal.

Rae didn't feel much like eating, but she fixed herself a bite once she got back home. She hopped onto her laptop and occupied herself with work for another five or six hours, most of it spent trying to make her brain play catch-up with her fingers. As soon as seven o'clock showed up, she couldn't fight it anymore. Rae eased onto her couch, and she went to sleep within a minute.

Rae had no idea how long she had been out, but it must have been for several hours because the darkness surrounded her now. What she did know for sure was that it was all happening again. Her chest rose and fell heavily in laborious rhythms, and her eyes jittered behind their lids. She was flat on her back, one arm hanging off the couch. Her body received a shockwave of fresh hysteria, and there wasn't a goddamn thing she could do about it. She couldn't even cry, which is what she wanted to do more than anything else. This must have been what it felt like to be buried alive.

Some time passed before there was any progress, but it was big when it came. Her eyes flinched open, and she could see the living room. The moon cast enough light to make out shapes, but nothing specific. And worst of all, Rae realized that everything other than her eyes was still paralyzed. This sent a new chill of terror through her as she remained in her frozen state.

She tried to lift the arm that dangled from the couch.

Move, motherfucker, move.

She devoted every ounce of her energy toward that one, usually simple, endeavor. And then she heard a sound, faint at first but becoming louder. Her heart dropped to the floor of her stomach, a place that light would never reach. *Could* never reach. It was the door crying open. It was the "presence." It was the Intruder.

The rapping noise from the previous episode came again, and the yellow demon slipped into her peripheral vision, moving side to side like a crab. Rae could only detect its silhouette, but she didn't have to see anything else to know that it was making its way toward her. She hollered wordless wails as the Intruder jumped onto the couch and squirmed ever-so-carefully onto her stomach, then her chest. There was no way it could be Mr. Socks this time. She closed her eyes as the weight settled there, and a new, almost distant warble filled her ears.

And then, something happened. She didn't know if it was a miracle, but she also didn't know what else to call it if it wasn't. Her skin broke out in gooseflesh, and her limbs teemed with life. Her heart emerged from those lifeless depths and dispatched strength through every vessel of her trembling body. Her arms came together, grabbed hold of whatever was on top of her, and hurled it against the wall. There was an audible splatter as it hit, and Rae sprung to her feet. She hit the light switch.

This time, the Intruder didn't disappear. A trail of yellow slime waterfalled down the wall to where it lay on the floor. Rae got a good look at it for the first time. It was a small chimeric beast with an engorged body, at least six legs, and scaly, gangrenous skin that seemed to be shedding with each raspy breath it took. Goatlike horns jutted above its eyeless sockets. It glared at her, gurgling and pissed off, trying to regain its footing.

Rae screamed. Her first instinct was to run away, but she didn't. She ran right at the Intruder and pounced on it, hearing at least one of its legs snap cleanly as she did so. She pushed down on it twice with both hands as if she were administering chest compressions to an unconscious person. Then she wrapped her fingers around its neck and began to strangle it. It felt hard and scabrous and disgusting to the touch. Yellow foam bubbled from its mouth, which carried four rows—two up top, two on the bottom—of jagged fangs that looked like shards of broken bone. It tried to fend her off with its good legs, but Rae's adrenaline high was too much in the moment. The Intruder's throaty song turned into a squeal as Rae looked into its gaping black eye sockets. Those circles were darker than any cavern in any corner of the world, she reckoned, and Rae couldn't bear them. She turned away.

Then a familiar voice came, and it hurt worse than anything had to this point. Rae's eyes fell upon the creature once more, but it no longer donned the hideous face of the Intruder. It now wore the broken face of Clem. Red water dribbled from its nose, and a blood-bloated goose egg distended about its left temple.

Rae's throat muscles locked up, and tears streamed down her cheeks.

The face whimpered. "Please don't do this to me, Rae," it pleaded. "No."

It blubbered. "Please don't do this to me, baby."

Rae shook her head, her grip easing a bit. "No," she said. "You're not you."

The face gulped. "Don't hurt me, Rae. I love you so much."

Rae coughed a painful sob. "You're not my Clementine!"

But the voice sounded like Clem, even as choked as it was. And its face was furrowed and pitiful. "Don't let me die again," it begged.

"Shut up!" Rae screamed.

"I don't wanna go back in the dark."

"Shut up! Shut up! Shut up!"

After another few seconds, it did. Its eyes closed and its body turned limp in Rae's hands. She collapsed next to it there on the floor, sobbing. She had held Clem's face at the ballpark, at the hospital in the Intensive Care Unit, and now she had held its throat and crushed its windpipe with so much malice and pain. Another moment or so passed before she curled up beside it, and there was something she hadn't noticed before. She drew closer. The Intruder still had Clem's face, but it reeked of this putrid, haunting odor. It stunk like evil and rotten flesh, and it stunk like guilt, and Rae had had enough of that for one lifetime. It didn't smell anything like Clem.

Rae sat up. She began scooting backward when the creature suddenly resumed the Intruder's face. It sprang to life, opened its maw of fangs, and lunged at Rae. She seized it by the neck again, and this time, she didn't let go. She picked it up like a small dog and slammed it on the ground once, twice. Up and then back down. On the third time, it exploded into a sizzling yellow pulp.

Rae crawled to the wall on the opposite side of the room and cupped her hand over her mouth. The demon's head was the only part of its body that remained, and it now lay in a puddle that looked like a giant paint spill. Rae stared at it for quite a spell as she tried to get her breathing under control and think of a way she could logically understand this. But there wasn't one. Dr. Pender had said that she didn't believe in physical demons, but that she did believe in other kinds. With her eyes now locked on the mess on her living room floor, Rae reckoned that, personally, she believed in a little bit of both.

The night's dream came and went in an unmemorable flourish, like a passerby on a busy street. Rae breathed. She awakened gradually, naturally, and shook the sleep out of her shoulders as she rolled over and stretched. The sheets felt cool and agreeable on her skin. She still had a few more hours to log, but she was well on her way to a restful night. She reached for the other side of the bed, but no one was there. And that was okay. It would have to be okay.

Rae threw the sheets back and wrapped herself in the tacky bathrobe. She yawned as she walked into the kitchen, poured herself a glass of water, and made it disappear in two gulps. She went into the living room where it all had happened and gazed at the wall for a minute or two. Most of the stain had come out, but not all of it. She still didn't know how she was going to explain that one to her mother when she came over for Christmas.

Rae opened the sliding door at the back, and the mellow tumble of the ocean poured into the house. She stood on the balcony for a minute or two, arms crossed, lapping up the salty fall air. And, of course, she picked up the subtlest hint of Clem's perfume. Below, the sand was gritty and cold. Above, the moon was three-quarters full; it sent steely shivers through the water and glowed dreams into Rae's eyes. The sleepless kind, but she didn't mind that. Not at all.

Devil Like You

It's a strange thing to accept that you're going to Hell.

Benji Crane reckoned he would be there in less than half an hour. He had been warned about the penance for unjustifiably taking another life. And, perhaps more so, for taking his own. He stared at the primed syringes on the counter and imagined how he would drift away like a skiff in a vast, rolling ocean. That is, if it worked. First, the unconsciousness. Then the paralysis. Then the cardiac arrest—his heart coming to a stop like a train screeching, braking toward the platform of its final destination. And then The Judgment. Standing there where it all began in the dimness of the after-hours, he closed his eyes. Then he heard it again.

"Don't forget your last meal, Mister," the voice said, a mangled echo in a tunnel with no light and no end.

Benji didn't think it was a bad first gig for a slick-behind-the-ears kid right out of pharmacy school. He swirled some Duke's mouthwash in a decanter as he leaned against the wall, a scruffy-cheeked, sallow-eyed man who was so slight he looked like a magic trick. The French Broad Drug & Sundry was a little mom-and-pop joint in unincorporated Bouley, a fifteen-minute drive from Black Mountain, North Carolina. Inside, some indistinguishable honky-tonk melody crackled through the intercom above as here-and-there patrons browsed the aisles with no intention of actually buying anything. Outside, the worst wildfires in a hundred years licked the mountainside foliage high into the distance from the Pisgah Forest to Woodfin.

The old lady on the other side of the counter hacked and wheezed with a force that brought water to her eyes. "You know I used to think they was full of it when they said these was the last days," she said. "But I'm starting to see the writing on the wall."

Benji dropped the bottle into a small paper bag and handed it to her. "Don't you mind all that, now," he said. "Just use this with your antibiotic, and you'll mend fine."

She adjusted her wool scarf and offered him the best smile her thin lips could muster as she waddled off toward the front of the store. Benji filed her rumpled prescription into the Rolodex with the others and drummed at the counter, looking for something to keep his mind occupied amidst the midday lull. He wouldn't find anything until a Federal Express courier dragged her way toward the pharmacy some fifteen minutes later, a fancy blue-and-red 8 × 11.5 envelope in tow. Benji wondered what it could be. He hadn't placed a special order for a customer in weeks, and it couldn't be the vendor shipment. No, that was another two days away.

"Afternoon," Benji said in an awkward croak, his gaunt wrist flicking toward some semblance of a wave.

The courier, an attractive woman of similar age, countered with a reserved nod and a clipboard.

Benji patted the pockets of his trousers before drawing a pen from his white coat, which cloaked his slender frame like bedsheets on a spook at Halloween. He blushed and laughed. "Anything good?" he asked as he signed.

She didn't say anything.

"Maybe it's some rain," Benji said. "Lord knows we need it." It sounded even lamer out loud than it had in his head. He didn't know why he couldn't be smooth like Slim Ray, the cool-handed, cigarette-smoking detective from the graphic novel series he was so fond of. Slim always had something badass to say or some solution for getting out of a pickle.

But mum was the word again with the courier. She pointed to the faded stamp superimposed over the shipping label of the envelope; in block letters, it read: **CONFIDENTIAL**. Benji took it from her, frowned a little, and tipped his head as she went on her way. He retreated to the corner of the pharmacy by the controlled substance cabinets and opened it with his pocketknife. The envelope contained four sheets of double-bonded paper. The first was marked **Memorandum** in heavy type, and the letterhead bore the insignia of Central Prison in Raleigh. The paragraphs beneath went as follows:

Mr. Crane,
    In accordance with state law, you have been randomly selected from a registry of compounding pharmacists to assist in the adjudicated sentence of G. Wayne Renart, inmate no. 11938. It is the opinion of Guilford County Circuit Court Judge Erich Hamby and the State of North Carolina that G. Wayne Renart should be put to death by lethal injection for the charge of murder in the first degree, three counts, effective 12:00 a.m. Nov. 23, 1991.
    Henceforth, your instructions are:
    Collect the following drugs and dosages: sodium pentothal 10 g; pancuronium bromide 200 mg; and potassium chloride 200 mEq. Secure these contents in an airtight container and package them in a Federal Express parcel. Mark "Urgent" and "Confidential," and ship to the prison infirmary no later than 12:00 p.m. Nov. 16. You'll find the mailing address provided at the foot of this document. Thereafter, you are to report to Central Prison, where you will receive further instructions, no later than 9:00 p.m. Nov. 22.
    Attached to this document are copies of the judgment of death and state statute, respectively. Furthermore, you'll find a copy of your rights, as well as the terms and conditions of your participation. Therein, you have twenty-

```
four hours to submit your acceptance or re-
fusal of participation in writing via telefax
in accordance with state law.
     God save the great state of North Carolina
and her sacred justice system.

Regards,
Clarence Morton
Warden - Nov. 9, 1991
```

Benji clutched the paper, heavy in his hands, and whipped his head around in search of the punchline to this tasteless joke. But he found no Candid Camera television crew. He sat down, folding his legs like a schoolchild, and placed the memorandum on the floor in front of him. He rocked back and forth and repeated the words as if their ink would vanish or morph into something less horrific. He discovered some comfort in the last sentence, but not much. After ten minutes passed, he rose to his feet and looked at the clock, and for once, he hoped the hours would drip through the day like wet sand through an old hourglass.

Benji stepped out into Main Street just before dark, the setting sun overhead blotted out by low-hanging swaths of grayish-white. The smoke in Bouley was omnipresent, drifting into town from the surrounding woods and shrouding the air, thick and bitter for miles upon miles in all directions. To make matters worse, it hadn't rained in weeks. In the distance, State Forestry helicopters dumped thousands of gallons of water and borate. They had done so twice daily for the better part of a month. But the slow, sweeping infernos always briefly smoldered before raging hungrier than before. There were no answers, only theories: Some said it was arson; some said it was a careless cigarette cast into the rain-deprived leaves of a historically dry fall season; some attributed it to the hellhound legends indigenous to these parts; others said it was God Himself, rendering His final verdict on a wicked world.

Benji cranked his two-tone pickup, his lungs seething from the mere walk across the street. With a little more than two hours until closing time, he made the drive to the library at Black Mountain College. At every local landmark he passed—from Grossman's Quiltery to Lowell's General Store to the strip mall out by Old Highway 70—someone looked at him as though they knew what kind of letter he had nestled in his breast pocket. And a paranoia wriggled into his shoulders as if he were taking a body out into the woods to bury it.

He parallel-parked, checked his rearview mirror one last time, and exited his truck in a beeline for the library doors. He hadn't been here since a time in his life when he could only afford to check out the latest Slim Ray adventure, and that was a good six or seven volumes ago. The common area was pokier than he remembered—thronged with patrons who had never quite made it out of the late sixties and college kids with their big headphones plugged into their cassette tape players alike. After a trip to the archives section, Benji set up shop at a microfiche reader tucked in the back left corner. He spent close to an hour yawning and surfing through clippings from the *Greensboro News & Record*. He started in 1981, and by 1984 he was close to closing out his tab. But when **Greensboro Postman Poisons Wife, Two Daughters** popped across the screen in bold monospaced font three slides later, Benji frantically twisted the dial to zoom in. He read each sentence of the front-page article twice.

Kirkwood:

A northside mail carrier is in police custody after authorities linked him to an August house fire that killed his wife and two young daughters.

Greensboro D.A. Dwight Becker says George Wayne Renart, 41, has been charged with three counts of first-degree murder and is being held without bond in the Guilford County Jail.

"This is a grisly, cold-blooded crime whose equal I've never seen in my 20 years of private and public service," Becker said. "We're confident that when all the evidence materializes, there will be a clear-cut path to justice for the loved ones of the victims."

Authorities say Renart, a 13-year employee of the

United States Postal Service, sedated his wife and children with lethal amounts of the anxiety drug Diazepam shortly after dinner on August 3 before setting the family home on fire and fleeing across the state to his mother's residence in Asheville. Arraignment for the defendant will be announced in the coming days.

This is a developing story.

Benji leaned back in his chair and heaved a sigh he had been holding in for hours. He scrolled on until the lights were dimmed and he found himself mostly alone. An article in early 1986 provided the most pertinent information yet:

New Details Emerge in Greensboro Mailman Murders

Guilford County Courthouse:

New information is being disclosed in the ongoing testimony against G. Wayne Renart, the Greensboro mailman charged with killing his wife, Bethany, and their two daughters before burning down their Kirkwood home in 1984.

Prosecutors say the defendant dosed his family with Valium, a drug his personal doctor had recently prescribed to him for insomnia, around 7:30 p.m. on Friday, August 3. By 8:15 p.m., Renart had torched their ranch-style rambler and was on his way to Asheville.

Renart previously told police that he had been at the home of his mother, Sheila Renart, for hours leading up to the blaze, citing a fight with his wife, after which she had kicked him out the previous day. The defense alleges that Bethany Renart had likely fallen asleep with a cigarette in her mouth.

The most recent testimony follows a particularly contentious day in court, with perhaps the most startling revelations coming from witnesses for the prosecution. The first witness, whose name was not immediately available, claims to have seen Mr. Renart creeping around the home shortly before seeing smoke. The second witness, a trustee of Mrs. Renart's estate, alleges that his client had appointed the defendant as a joint beneficiary of a pending inheritance estimated in the upper hundreds of thousands of dollars in the weeks leading up to the murders.

Benji's skin began to crawl like a vine.

"Pardon me, sir," a reedy voice trailed from behind him.

Benji jerked forward as if someone had sprung out from the corner of a sketchy alleyway and screamed "Boo!" He pushed an open palm against his chest, realizing he had startled the librarian more than she had startled him.

She folded her hands. "We'll be closing in fifteen minutes."

Benji nodded. Then he read on:

"[Renart] hadn't banked on the bodies being retrieved before they were charred beyond acceptable conditions for toxicology tests," lead prosecutor T.A. Broughton, Jr. told the *News & Record.* "But this evidence is damning. We have nothing but faith in the jurors to do what's right."

The defense maintains that Mrs. Renart was a drug abuser and negligent mother. According to Edwin Ball, Mr. Renart's attorney, Bethany Renart medicated her children with pills she had stolen from her husband after taking some for herself. The neighbor, a key witness for the prosecution, has been diagnosed with early onset dementia, Ball claims. No explanation has been given for the trust fund.

"It's shameless, the lengths [the defense] will go to just to protect a monster," Broughton said. "We take solace in knowing that God will have the last word on this."

The jury is set to hear closing arguments next week.

Benji combed through a few more films as the seconds ticked down to ten o'clock. He panned in on the end of an article entitled, **Renart Found Guilty of Triple-Homicide**, and read the last two sentences aloud:

For the murder of Bethany Renart, the jury recommended a life sentence without parole. For the murders of Rachel and Jacquelyn Renart, the jury recommended death.

He buried his eyes into his hands and massaged his forehead until he could feel the presence of the librarian approaching behind him yet again.

Benji exited the building as it was darkened and stood on the sidewalk in the harsh, endless fog for several moments. He breathed in and imagined billows of smoke entering his lungs. Then he imagined that same smoke entering the lungs of a young mother. He imagined two little girls choking on those same plumes. And he thought he might suffocate. He climbed into his truck and gasped. "Let's think this through," he said. "It's not like you'd be firing the bullet or switching on the juice to the electric chair. You'd be prepping the drugs, that's it. You didn't take a Hippocratic Oath. You're not an MD."

Wringing his steering wheel like a sponge, Benji went back and forth with himself. He had made it almost three decades without developing an opinion, one way or the other, on capital punishment. Besides, Renart was condemned to death anyway. If Benji didn't offer his services, surely someone else would. But who would he be to potentially prolong this and deprive an innocent woman and her two small children of justice? He couldn't have that on his conscience. He had nieces and nephews of his own. Benji turned the key in the ignition. There had only been three lethal injections in state history. Pulling out into the mountain night, Benji Crane decided he would be part of the fourth.

The walls at Central Prison were almost white—tinted with an eggshell tone as if to soften them up and render them less blinding. Benji had arrived at the chain-link and barbed wire of the east gate at a quarter before nine. From there, he had been escorted in by a sleepy-eyed guard who looked rather indifferent given the occasion of the evening.

Benji stood just inside the double doors beyond the metal awning—where he assumed the ambulance would pick up the body later—while a group of important-looking people checked his credentials in the next room. He stared at those almost-white walls as if he could see past them. He had come sporting his lab coat, a dryer-fluffed oxford shirt, and a pair of slacks, but he couldn't help thinking an executioner's mask might have been more appropriate.

Once the vetting was complete, the same lethargic guard, now accompanied by another, led Benji down a long and narrow corridor. A dozen or so holding cells were on either side, but it didn't look like anyone inhabited them. Benji peered into one of the eye hatches and found it completely void of light. That was when he realized he was under the same roof as Wayne Renart. The night had been brisk, but Benji made up his mind that it was even colder in here. He didn't think that was a coincidence. The three men hung a hard right through one last set of doors into a tight room consumed mostly by counter-space. A curtain occluded the lone window, and on the other side was where Benji figured "it" would all go down. He had heard rumors that the death chamber in Raleigh was boxier than most, and if it was any smaller than the room in which he currently stood, he knew that they were true.

The two guards exited the room and were replaced by a fat, bespectacled old man whose tan suit was at least a decade beyond its sell-by date. He had strips of steely hair where locks probably hadn't been for thirty years, and when he shook Benji's hand, his second chin jiggled like a water balloon. "You must be Crane," he said. "And if you ain't, boy, are you in the wrong goddamn place." He laughed with a smoker's cackle.

"Yessir."

"Good," the man said, picking up on his new acquaintance's uncomfortableness. "I'm Warden Morton. Seeing as how you're here, I take it my letter found you okay."

Benji nodded. "I faxed your office."

"Right. Well, then, sparing any more suspense, I'm here for your 'further instructions.'" He balled his fist and rapped the counter with it as he talked. "I've presided over every injection death in this state. I ran my first three tighter than a nun's ass, and they were gravy, each and every one. This'n will be no different. Your only job is to prep the syringes—one per drug—and another set of each as a backup in case one of my employees shits the bed."

"What dosages?"

"Shitfire, don't you know? You're the pharmacist."

Benji looked confused.

Morton grinned. "I'm just yanking you." He reached into his breast pocket and pulled out a key. "Here," he said, handing it to Benji. "The drugs are in that cabinet along with an SOP. Return everything, lock up, and hand this back to me before you leave. I'll be just outside there."

"That's it?"

Morton adjusted his bifocals. "That'll do her. My personnel deploys the drugs. We have a doc on standby to pronounce death. All clear?"

"Yessir," Benji said, a lump forming in his throat.

Morton exited the room and shut the door behind him. Benji ran his fingertips over the grooves of the key and tried to keep his mind from wandering to what would be happening in the next room in an hour and a half. He unlatched the cabinet and found a list of directions along with the drugs he had shipped a week earlier. Carefully, he drew each one of them into its own syringe, mindful of his own shaky hands. He tried not to picture those same hands being bound by thick leather straps. He tried not to visualize himself writhing on a gurney, snoring, spewing gibberish, and likely shitting himself. The heart monitor coding. Instead, he labeled each barrel, separated them, and arranged them on the counter as advised. With one last look, he returned the empty vials to the cabinet, locked it, and left the room. Just outside, Morton was eyeballing his wristwatch.

"Here you go," Benji said, relinquishing the key.

Morton smiled and gestured toward a guard just down the hall. "Amos, see this gentleman out, will you?"

The walk back to his truck was a lot shorter than the walk from it. The old banger was waiting for him just outside the prison awning.

The State had offered to put him up in a decent hotel for the night, but Benji thought it was probably best to put as much distance between himself and Central Prison as possible. It began to sleet as he headed down Western Boulevard toward Interstate 40, but he didn't mind that. All he could think about was that quote from the Bhagavad Gita that Oppenheimer had popularized after Hiroshima and Nagasaki. How did it go? "I am become Death, the destroyer of worlds"? Yeah, that must've been it.

Benji was nearly fifty miles into his trip when something came over him. Not quite a pain, but more of a pressure. It gripped at his chest and wouldn't let go. He doubled over, one hand still on the wheel, and clutched at his sternum like a football player who's just had his wind knocked out. A heart attack at twenty-eight? Couldn't be. He toyed with pulling over into the breakdown lane, but the sensation subsided over the next few minutes. He looked up at the clock. It read: 12:03.

"What have I done?"

Benji asked this question to no one in particular over the next week of restless nights as he sat hunched over in the moonshine at the edge of his bed. While others were enjoying Thanksgiving festivities with their friends and family, Benji shut himself out from the rest of the world when he could and leafed through a familiar copy of *Slim Ray* when he had the mind to do so. An uneasy feeling followed him like a bad cold he couldn't shake, so much so that he called out of work for the first time in his life. When he returned, there was a pile of work to catch up on and not nearly enough hours in the day to do it. That night, he lingered around the pharmacy until half-past ten, filing an insurance claim here, nibbling at a bland canned tuna sandwich there. That's when he first heard it. It was the same sound his boyhood dog Tripp had made just before it limped off to die alone in the crawl space under the house.

Benji spun around wildly to locate it, but he couldn't. The building was dark, save for the light of his workstation lamp. "Who's there?"

he asked.

The whimpering escalated into sobbing, and it seemed to bounce from one side of the room to the next.

Benji whipped out his pocketknife and wielded it around. Then the same sensation he had experienced on his way back from Raleigh embraced him again, like that one relative at the family reunion who always hugs past their welcome. He winced and hurled an unconvincing warning: "I'll—I'll have the sheriff over here in no time."

The sobbing gave way to syllables, muffled at first, but increasingly clearer—albeit slanted and distorted. "Why'd you do it to me, Mister?"

"What—what're you talking about?" Benji asked, the words creeping into his throat like puke.

"I didn't do nothing, Mister. Why'd you have to do it to me?"

Benji opened his mouth to repeat his question, but a subzero waft of air descended upon the room, stealing his words. The wan, grainy figure of a man quickened from the darkness and into the light. He was comparable in height to Benji, but slightly thicker in the bones—if he had any bones. He wore the pigeon blue of the USPS and a sun helmet that cut right above eyes so narrow they looked like the holes on a pegboard. A small, cartoonish tattoo of a coyote dwelt on his forearm, a shit-eating grin plastered on its poorly illustrated face.

Benji fell to the floor and scooted backward as the thing approached him. It seemed to glide rather than walk, an aura slithering about it that Benji likened to the smoke on the other side of the walls.

"What do you want? Drugs? Money?" Benji asked, even though he suspected that the man hovering above him was interested in neither.

The man stopped and sniffled. "No, Mister. I've had my share of drugs. And you're the one give 'em to me."

Benji didn't immediately understand. But looking into those shrunken eyes, the epiphany dawned on him, sour and pitiless. He had gotten the heebie-jeebies plenty of times around campfires in the Scouts, but by the time his teenage years rolled around, he'd figured ghosts existed solely in the reels of thirty-five-millimeter film. That was until he stared up at the woeful posture of Wayne Renart.

"You killed an innocent man," Renart said, flecks of snot and tears dribbling from his chin.

"No."

"You did!" the apparition screamed as he burst into another round of waterworks.

Benji shuffled backward until his body rested against the wall. "You're not real."

"Oh yeah?" Renart dove to the floor and slid until an inch at most separated his face from Benji's. "This real enough for you, Mister?" His breath reeked like carrion under the hottest of summer suns.

Benji gulped. "You murdered your wife. You murdered those girls. I wouldn't have gone through with it unless I was sure of that."

Renart shook his head.

"You wanted that money all to your lonesome."

"No, sir."

"You're lying."

"No, sir!" Renart said as he rose to a standing position. He backpedaled a few paces. "I never laid a bad finger on their pretty little heads. I'm guilty of plenty, that much I don't renounce. But not murder."

"Is this the part where you say not yet?" Benji asked.

Renart's eyes danced. "No, sir. I'm not gonna kill you. Not me. I ain't no devil."

Benji tried to regulate his breathing—in through his nose, out through his mouth. "I suppose you want me to believe this was one of those wrong-place-wrong-time deals, huh?"

"I was set up, Mister. No two ways about it." Renart grew detached, almost hypnotized. "You don't believe me yet, but you will directly."

"Even if that's true, I'm not the one who stuck the needle in your arm."

"Blood's on your hands, all the same."

"So you are gonna kill me, ain't you?"

Renart slipped deeper into his trance. He droned on for several seconds in a strange tongue before skidding back into his own. "When I say unto the wicked, Thou shalt surely die; and thou givest him not warning, nor speakest to warn the wicked from his wicked way to save his life; the same wicked man shall die in his iniquity; but his blood I will require at thine hand."

Benji recognized the scripture, but years separated him from the first time he had heard it. Old Testament, he reckoned but wasn't sure. One thing he was sure of: This whole situation hadn't sat well with him, and now, for the first time, he genuinely felt like he had made a terrible mistake. The ghost of Wayne Renart dropped to its knees some five feet away. It began to gurgle as it trembled and flickered back toward the dark. It squeezed its throat, black liquid spurting from its gaping mouth. Then the same black liquid streamed from its eyes in skinny streaks. And as it reached toward the ceiling with a quivering, outstretched hand, it dissipated before Benji's eyes without a trace.

Benji didn't move at first. But once he had convinced himself that he hadn't been dreaming, he dropped his head. He cried with no tears to show for it. The weight of the subsequent darkness pressed down on his shoulders and whispered into his ears.

"Sometimes," his old man would say with a voice deeper than still waters, "an eye for an eye just don't cut it."

Benjamin Crane Sr.'s stories about justice in the jungles of Vietnam often provided relevant commentary for his son's own life. This was one of those times. Benji had taken an eye—maybe with good intentions—but he had taken one nonetheless. Wayne Renart had died, slowly and in the dark, and Benji supposed the atonement for his part would be twofold. If he really had helped to kill a falsely convicted man, that is. The specter had been sorrowful, not vengeful. It had declared innocence, not vows of retribution. Even so, Benji spent the next forty-eight hours on pins and needles, waiting for it to collect on its unfinished business. He knew he couldn't go to the police. They would laugh him up one side of the Tennessee border and back down the other.

Maybe they would slap a straitjacket on him, toss him into a wagon, and ship him out to the mental hospital at Dix Hill. Maybe that's what he needed.

"You ill?" one customer asked.

"You look right pale," another observed.

"Don't look like he's took a shower in a week," a coworker whispered to another.

Benji shrugged them all off—said he felt like shit because the smoke outside was causing his asthma to fester. He didn't have asthma.

On the first morning of December, three days after the paranormal encounter, Benji's supervising pharmacist strolled in, took one look at him, and told him to take the rest of the day off. Benji was the type who never put in for vacation, but this time, he did so without a fight. Once he had departed, he hopped on the Blue Ridge Parkway from Old Highway 70 and cruised until the arrow on his fuel gauge lounged just above the E. He pulled over at the Walnut Cove Overlook, one of his favorites, and swayed back and forth at its edge.

The mountains, in all their snow-crowned majesty, would have been breathtaking on any normal day, even to someone who was no stranger to them, but now smoke blanketed them like a film of filth. The solace Benji usually found at three thousand feet came to him wrapped as the grayest of miseries. He gazed out into the fleecy veils with equally gray eyes, and for a moment, he wondered what it would be like to leap into them and let them take him away. Then he heard a rustle behind him. He turned. What had started as a soft crackle of limbs became the snapping song of bones being broken as Wayne Renart waded through the dead leaves and branches at the fringe of the overlook.

Benji sighed. "Just get it over with," he said, turning back toward the dreary void stretching before him.

Renart came to a standing stop next to him. His cheeks were stained with the same inky substance as they had been when he vanished in the pharmacy. He was dressed the same as well, but this time, he lugged an old canvas satchel with him. He moaned softly. "No, no," he said. "I ain't gonna kill you. I told you, I ain't no devil."

"Then why're you here? What do you want from me?"

Renart didn't speak again for a minute. "You ever heard of the In-Between, Mister?" He finally answered in a monotone cadence. Black tears began to climb his cheeks, slip into his beady eyes, and leak through his open mouth.

Benji shuddered at the sight. "What do you mean?"

"The In-Between. Not Heaven. Not Hell."

"You mean Purgatory?"

"If you wanna call it that," Renart said.

"I reckon I have. One version or another."

"That's where I am right now," Renart said. "Lost and stranded in limbo. Not knowing if I'm coming or going. You know what it's like, Mister? To feel like all the joy's been sucked up out of you like the smoke from a cigarette? All that's left is the ashes."

"Maybe that's your punishment." Benji turned, but Renart wasn't there.

"Not for a crime I didn't commit," Renart said from Benji's other side.

Benji jumped. "Jesus!"

"My apologies."

Benji struggled to catch his wind. "If not you, then who?"

"When my wife's mama died, her brother was a Godsend. I reckon he thought that'd make up for all the years he was in and out of the joint instead of being there. But when the family lawyer told him he'd been cut out of the will, well, he stopped being such a Godsend. Money does terrible things to people."

"What are you saying?" Benji asked.

"That monster." Renart started to cry again. "He took my babies from me." The sides of his satchel bubbled and pulsed as a hazy wisp curled from its flap. He opened it and withdrew a glistening black orb.

Benji backed up.

"See for yourself."

A cylindrical rod of light spilled from the orb and manifested into moving images. It reminded Benji of the picture cast by one of those old movie projectors he had worked on during summer gigs at the Bouley Theater. Everything played out before his eyes in flashes. He saw Renart squirming in the death chamber at Central Prison. He saw Renart shackled by his feet in a courtroom, and before that, ducking into the back of a police cruiser with a disoriented look on his face. He saw Renart weeping on a church pew. Then he saw a man who wasn't Renart dousing a living room floor with gasoline and sparking it with a Zippo lighter.

Benji turned from the images in agony, tears welling in his eyes like a dam on the verge of collapse. He crouched down and drew a fist to his puckered lips, knowing he would get sick.

Renart deposited the orb into his satchel and squatted beside him. "Why? Why'd you have to do it to me, Mister?"

"But the neighbor saw you," Benji said.

"That man was an old coot," Renart replied. "Died from Alzheimer's a few years later."

Benji bit back sobs. "I'm—I'm so sorry."

"That don't cut it."

"Then what?"

Renart whispered, "Set me free."

"How?" Benji asked.

"You gotta even the score."

"Kill myself?"

Renart didn't answer. He didn't have to.

Benji wiped his sweaty hands across the knees of his khakis and dipped his head. "Then what happens to me?"

"That, I cain't say," Renart said, his voice sprawling off. "That's between you and someone else."

The next time Benji looked up, Renart was gone. The young pharmacist rose to his feet on wobbly legs. If only he were Slim Ray. Then he would know what to do. In the most recent release, Slim had discovered that his partner had betrayed him, and in true Slim fashion, said something really pithy before exacting his revenge accordingly. But Benji wasn't Slim Ray. He was a whimpering nerd-man, studying the sloping drop of the overlook. He tried to do the math on how long he would be conscious and how much he'd feel. He considered evening the score right then and there. But something stopped him. He jumped into his truck and motored back down the Parkway toward Asheville.

He rang the doorbell of the little house with the terracotta roof that looked out of place amongst the other homes on the Weaverville-Asheville line. He had gotten the address out of the *White Pages* of a phone booth in the Bouley Ingles parking lot and held onto it for several days, never expecting he would really use it. But there he was, going over his spiel in his head as he stared at the rotted wooden trellis dressing the front porch wall. A pint-sized old lady with gauzy hair answered and squinted at him through the wire netting of the storm door.

"Missus Renart?" Benji asked.

"Yeah, who's asking?" she questioned with an Appalachian lilt.

"My name's Paul Sloop; I'm a writer for the *Bouley Beat*," Benji began, trying to smooth out the creases in his voice. "I know it must be a hard time for you, but I was hoping you'd be so kind as to let me ask you a few questions about your son."

Her face furrowed as she drummed at her doorway with shriveled fingers. "Most of the newspaper and TV people have already been by."

"Yes, ma'am, I can appreciate that. I'm just doing a short follow-up piece. I'd only take up a few minutes of your time."

"I've got a lot of that these days," she said, swinging the creaking door open. "Come on in."

Benji did as he was told, hugging a composition notepad to his belly.

"What paper you say you was with?" she asked as she led him into a cozy living room.

"*The Bouley Beat*."

"Huh," she said. "Ain't never heard of them."

"We're new."

She offered Benji a seat on the orange-and-brown flannel couch. He took it, somewhat surprised his ruse had actually worked. The real Paul Sloop had been a classmate of his in pharmacy school, much more handsome and sure of himself than he. Suddenly, Benji realized he would be winging it from here, and his mouth became dry.

Sheila Renart, widowed mother of only child George Wayne, slumped into a recliner on the other side of the room. "I got used to your kind in the beginning and through the trial," she said. "Not so much in the last few years. But y'all come running about the second week of November."

"We're short-staffed, so we pony off the *Citizen-Times* a lot," Benji explained, the blades of a ceiling fan overhead drowning out most of his voice. He said louder, "But this one I wanted to do for myself."

"All right, what do you wanna know?"

Benji paused. "Were you there in Raleigh on the twenty-second?"

"No, sir," she said, rocking back and forth. "I ain't been out there once since they put him away."

"Why?"

"Never cared to see my own flesh and blood caged up like some kind of animal, truth-be-told. I wrote him on holidays."

Benji doodled with his pencil, pretending to take notes. In the background, some matinee judge show played out on the television set. Benji thought it was strange considering how much of that Sheila Renart had probably been through in real life. He scooched down the couch toward the television, where a photograph of a younger Wayne Renart sat atop a crocheted skirt. His smile gleamed right through the black-and-white matte. Something wasn't right about it.

"That ain't what you really come to find out, though, is it?" she asked.

"Ma'am?"

She stopped rocking. "You come to find out what they all come to find out: whether or not he was really here with me when it all happened. I knew it the second I seen you standing there on my porch."

Benji rested his notepad on his lap and interlaced his fingers. "Was he?"

She leaned forward. "I'll tell you what I told that judge and that jury

107

from the stand: He was here. Him and Beth got into it the day before, and he come down here after work that evening. Spent most of his time in the spare bedroom yonder. I ain't never told a lie outside of a white one. I'm a Christian woman."

"Yes, ma'am," Benji said.

She slouched back. She seemed cold and unmoved. Maybe she had grown numb to it all. Benji guessed seven years could do that to someone.

"Well, I'll be getting on my way," Benji said.

Sheila Renart nodded. She led Benji to the front porch and lingered for a moment.

Just as Benji glanced into the front yard, Wayne Renart faded into being beside the roadside mailbox. This time, chains were wrapped about his wrists and ankles. He mouthed, "Help me." Benji closed his eyes. When he opened them, hundreds of pinholes surfaced on Renart's body at once. They oozed at first. Then they gushed. Then the liquid sprayed from them and into the road in all directions before he burst into a pulpy black puddle. Benji turned to Sheila Renart, a tear sliding down his cheek.

She hadn't seen. She had been looking at the smoky hellscape in the distance, the hard lines in her skin like the ridges in the mountains she mused on. "Was you raised in the good book?" she asked.

"Yes, ma'am."

"You know the Lord said he wouldn't destroy the world with water this time. But with fire."

Benji's last meal—if it could be called that—had been half a toaster pastry that morning.

But that was the last thing on his mind. He watched the two syringes in front of him as if they would miraculously slip through a wormhole and travel to some universe far, far away. He had been scared plenty of times in his life, but this was different. It wasn't the physical dying that got him as much as the prospect of the unknown. There was no guarantee that this would work. The drugs were supposed to be dispensed into the bloodstream sequentially in three separate shots. But given that the first would render him unconscious and unable to inject the next two, Benji had no choice but to take his chances and combine them all into one cocktail. He had even made a backup, probably just for shits and giggles. At best, it would be like someone turned out the lights. At worst, it wouldn't work, and he would live out the rest of his years an invalid.

"I'll pray for you," Wayne Renart said.

Benji didn't know what good that would accomplish. A big part of him still believed that he would have some explaining to do shortly. He peered over at Renart, who smiled an uncharacteristic smile; it was like the one worn by his coyote tattoo.

"Set me free, Mister," Renart whispered.

"You're sure this is the only way?"

"Yessir," Renart responded, his carrier satchel bouncing on his hip as he began to pace like a junkie. "I wish it wasn't, but it is."

Benji breathed in and out. In lieu of a proper tourniquet, he unhooked his belt, wrapped it around his bicep, and tugged at it with his teeth until a bulging vein sprouted under his skin. He plunged the needle into it, and grimacing, thumbed the liquid contents of the syringe into his body. After a moment, he lumbered backward with a stony face until the wall halted his progress. He slid down it until he was seated on the floor, gazing up at Renart with glassy eyes.

The ghost now beamed back at him with arched eyebrows, his satchel undulating. He pulled out his black orb. "I've got a package for you. A real good one."

He rolled the orb along the floor like a marble, and it stopped at Benji's feet. The ball threw its light, and moving pictures commenced on the pharmacy ceiling. Benji saw Renart in plainclothes, pulverizing pills and pouring them into glasses of milk and wine on a dinner table. He saw him hovering above the lifeless bodies of a woman and two children, the same twisted coyote grin whittled into his face. He saw him looking over his shoulder as he slinked around the burning house, and after that, driving at the speed limit on the interstate in an old station wagon. Then he saw him in the spare bedroom of his mother's mountain house, clutching his stomach as he howled soundless laughter on the bed.

Benji's lips coiled in horror.

Renart glided forward. "Die slow for me," he said in a bottomless voice.

Benji shivered where he sat. Then he twitched and convulsed, his heels clacking against the floor beneath.

"That's it," Renart said. "That's a good lad."

When Benji's eyelids closed and his body stopped moving several minutes later, Renart giggled. He frolicked around the pharmacy, dancing with an invisible partner and humming in a scratchy pitch. But just as his laughter began to taper off, Benji's limbs stirred. The young pharmacist's eyes popped open, and he pushed himself to his feet. He untangled the belt from his arm and spiked it on the ground.

Renart was dumbfounded. "Why aren't—you're supposed to be dead."

Benji held out the empty syringe. "Saline solution."

Renart didn't understand.

"Saltwater," Benji said. He grabbed the other syringe, the liquid inside glaring at the specter. "And behind door number two: the dog that bit you." He was surprised at how cool the words came out. Slim Ray resurrected.

Wayne Renart fell to his knees. "You sneaky sonofabitch."

"No," Benji said. "Not me. I'm no devil."

Renart fuzzed over like a television with rabbit ears in a storm. A thing being reduced, erased, unborn. That foul, scummy shit that seemed to weep from him slathered every inch of his facade now. He bitched and vomited and jabbered. Faded in and out. He hurled a guttural retch into the dim pharmacy, and an awful, hellish hollering from someone or something other than him followed as he was dragged through the floor of the French Broad Drug & Sundry. His residual aura spiraled overhead and dispersed into circulation with the rest of the conditioned air.

Benji exhaled. He emptied the remaining syringe into the sink and watched as it circled down the drain. He locked up and shoved a note under the door. It read:

Jeff, I think it's time I took you up on that extended vacation.

Thunder clapped above as he tossed his white coat into the bed of his truck, not caring if it would still be there the next time he checked. On his drive home, droplets of rain pricked at his windshield. Benji Crane couldn't be sure, but they looked like black tears.

Another Runner in the Night

Miguel didn't remember much of anything worth remembering from right before it happened. Nor did he have a mind for the distant past—his childhood, his hometown, the various rites of passage we all endure. It wasn't total amnesia, though all that remained seemed random and trivial.

But he recalled the event itself well enough:

He was nursing a beer on the couch, playing Super Smash Bros. Ultimate, his Jack Russell, Luis, curled up next to him. At first, he thought the explosion of light was from the gameplay, but it was too all-consuming for that. The room's pressure dropped dramatically, and a soundlessness fell over the night like ash in the aftermath of a volcanic eruption. He placed his controller on the cushion next to him, peeled the blinds open over his shoulder, but there was hardly anything discernible on the other side of the window. He had never witnessed such a brightness, and yet it didn't make him squint. He knew Luis was barking, but he couldn't hear him. He knew he had spilled the beer on the rug, but he didn't care.

Next, he was on the landing outside the back entrance of his second-floor apartment, staring at the light on the horizon with a skepticism he didn't have a precedent for. There was a bowl of cashed weed on the ledge beside a potted cactus. The craft itself was stationary, flat. It hovered above the mountains of the little coal town, an impossible turtle shell suspended in the sky, each scute ablaze with radiant hexagonal white moon rays of motion. Everything in the foreground was lost in a kind of anti-shadow: the old brick methodist church on the hill, the charming green Georgian house with the out-of-place tin roof, the falling stone wall that began at the parking lot across the street and ended at the police station a block over. To the best of Miguel's knowledge, nobody else was witnessing this with him; but from an open window at the historic hotel next to his building, he heard low music. It was "You Are—I Am" by Manfred Mann's Earth Band.

Somehow appropriate.

Miguel was well-read on religious experiences—at least he had been—though he couldn't really say he'd ever had one himself. He didn't think. By his recollection, most people reported feeling overcome with emotion, engulfed by sensations indescribable in their supernaturalness, but he was blank in a way that didn't seem feasible for someone alive. His ability to speak, to form and process simple thoughts, escaped him as he looked upon a sight that was someone's dream, someone else's nightmare. Time was a concept for fools in this reality. The object, perfect in its proportions, remained stock-still for an indeterminate amount of time, but eventually it began to move horizontally to the right, then vertically, then horizontally and vertically again—absurdly even and telegraphed in these actions. And when it was gone, seemingly at once, it was replaced by total blindness.

Without any explanation for how he had gotten there, Miguel found himself in the parking lot across the street, walking Luis under a starless expanse. Everything seemed accounted for in the world around him—the cars, the hedgerow along the back of the lot, the one lamp post that was always out. But the mysterious craft, the light, was gone. Miguel limped dumbly back to his apartment building through a cognitive fog, and it wasn't until he reached the base of the rotting exterior stairs that he realized Luis wasn't with him.

The next morning, still in a haze, Miguel got up at six o'clock without the aid of an alarm. He ate breakfast, a bar of unremarkable flavor, saddled up in his car, and started driving, though he didn't know what compelled him to do so. Nothing of his past had returned to him yet, so he let muscle memory guide his path to the bioprocessing plant on the town's industrial parkway, which housed only one other business—a mass producer of printer ink cartridges. He entered the plant, trying to make sense of it, an invisible force pulling him in just the right direction at just the right time. He turned up on a warehouse floor, maybe a dozen stainless steel cylindrical vats organized longwise in two rows before him. Fermentation vessels.

"Say hey, *Mijo*," a voice called from behind, and when Miguel turned toward it, he found an intense, muscular man of his mid-fifties approaching fast. One of the operators? Of course. And Miguel himself was one also, yes.

"How's it going?" Miguel offered weakly.

"It's going," the man replied. He had veins in his neck that other people didn't seem to have. Miguel tried to put a finger on who the man reminded him of, and suddenly he realized it was a wrestler from his boyhood, the Macho Man Randy Savage—but with shorter hair and minus the ridiculous sunglasses.

Miguel bided his time, hoping he would remember whatever it was he did here sooner than later. He wasn't even sure which state he was in. Virginia? North Carolina? Tennessee? Fuck if he knew.

"You all right, Mijo?" the man asked, abandoning a gauge he was tinkering with. *Mijo*. His pronunciation was on par with other white people. You know the kind. The ones who frequent Mexican restaurants but support a wall at the southern border.

"Yeah, I'm good..." Miguel began, trying his damndest to put a name to this face.

"Terry," another voice shouted from somewhere beyond the fermenters, as if on cue. "Come see me when you get a minute, will you?"

"You got it," the muscular man, apparently Terry, yelled back. "It's always something, am I right?" he said to Miguel, shaking his head.

Miguel agreed that it was. Slowly, he made his rounds, performing whatever minor maintenance he could as bits and pieces of know-how came crawling back. The fermentation vessels, with their shining metallic faces, brought to mind the events of the night before. The weightlessness, the vacuous nature of self, the unspeakable light. The unlikely immensity of the object. Down the line, Terry was humming something; it was surely "You Are—I Am" by Manfred Mann's Earth Band, a song whose title was still a mystery to Miguel at this point.

"Terry," Miguel said, making his way back toward his coworker.

"What's up, Mijo?"

"You didn't happen to notice anything strange last night, did you?"

Terry furrowed his brow, and then, as if it had just dawned on him that instant, he said, "I sure as shit did, man. Big helmet thing just floating there on top of the mountains, brighter than the fucking sun. Never seen anything like that in my life, man."

For a moment, Miguel was overcome with the greatest sense of relief. "I saw it, too. What do you make of it?"

"Aw, hell, Mijo, I didn't look at it for more than a second or two."

That might explain why he isn't suffering from the same amnesia, Miguel thought.

"I tried to call it into the country station down the road," Terry went on, hands stuffed under his vascular arms, the right bicep of which sported a tattoo of a murmillo gladiator, "but they thought I was just a tweaker, I reckon. There might be something about it in the paper today or tomorrow, if there's anything at all. They can say it come from the mines, but there hasn't been so much as a swinging dick out there in almost ten years. My theory?" He looked around. "Goddamn military."

Miguel nodded, trying to understand. "Well, whoever, whatever, it was, I think it spooked my dog. I can't find him. Her?"

"I'm sorry to hear that, Mijo," Terry said with a genuine expression of concern. "Poor Luis. I'm sure he'll turn up." He made like he was going to get back to it, but Miguel stopped him.

"Terry. You believe in UFOs?"

Terry let go of an uncomfortable laugh, something popping on his forehead. "Nah, man, I believe in things I can see," he said. "Like this cup of coffee that's got my name on it in the breakroom. But hey, I'm going to

Bible study tonight. Wanna join? Might help you take your mind off shit."

That night, the neighbors down the hall were having loud sex, and Miguel couldn't focus on anything else no matter how hard he tried. He smoked a fat bowl, gathered the missing pet posters he had printed at the plant, and exited the front of the apartment into the hot evening. He crossed to the boutique on the other side of the building—the one with the creepy window mannequins in their cheap prints—into a row of sleepy zelkovas that lined Main Street. The Christmas lights stayed up year-round here, on lamp posts and tree trunks; everywhere they hung, Miguel affixed a poster. The photo he had used was a good one from his phone, Luis wearing a blue-and-orange conical hat, looking unimpressed behind a cake Miguel had ordered for him at a now-bankrupt organic dog bakery two towns over. Specific memories of Luis were lost on Miguel, but that didn't stop his heart from hurting. From longing for his special boy, his only friend.

After he had put up twenty or thirty posters from his stack, Miguel wandered along the darkened storefronts hunting a newspaper receptacle. He found one in front of the deserted furniture store, reached in, and took a copy. There was news of a shakeup on the local school board; a large donation to the community hospital; a person injured during a fireworks display. But nothing of UFOs. Miguel was briefly heartened by the image of a spaceship in the bottom-left corner of the front page, but it was just a used car dealership advertising "out of this world" pricing. He turned around, alone on this self-contained plane, and headed back toward his apartment. If there were sounds, the mountains kept them secret.

He was almost back when the phone vibrated in his pocket, an unsaved number. Miguel swiped to answer it, held it to his ear, breathed into the receiver.

A voice breathed back, and then it said, "Mijo."

"Terry?" Miguel said. Perhaps, he thought, his coworker was ill about being stood up for Bible study.

"I think I'm bleeding from my ears, man," Terry said.

"That's not good."

"I'll keep you posted," Terry said. And then he hung up.

Miguel imagined blood running down Terry's meaty neck like candle wax as he sat wherever he sat, eating a Hungry Man microwavable dinner, or something like that. Probably watching YouTube videos about conspiracies or else movies with Russell Crowe in them. Washing down gas station dick pills with a canned energy drink. How full of poison was his mind?

When Miguel rejoined the now, he was standing in front of the boutique, and the rest of the missing posters were in a pile at his shoes. He lifted his eyes. There was a mannequin in cheetah, one in paisley. Then there was not a mannequin at all, but a person, frozen in a denim shirt-dress, hands on her hips, every feature of her pretty face stretched into a smile by invisible fingers. Her tremble, hardly noticeable. She looked beyond Miguel at nothing, tears glued to her jawline like they were forbidden from falling to the floor. A person locked inside her own body.

He watched her for a long time, heart in his throat.

In the breakroom at the plant, Terry's ear canals were packed with gauze. He chewed ravenously at a bologna and cheese sandwich, his second of the afternoon, as Miguel looked on, half bemused, half uncomfortable, his lunch a single cup of black coffee, now half full and cold. As soon as the oaf finished off the last corner of whitebread crust, he cocked his tree-trunk leg and cut an audible fart. Even if Miguel wanted to say something about it, which was a big if, he figured it would be wise to keep his opinions to himself on account of Terry looking like he could easily crack a Brazil nut in the ditch of his elbow.

"I'm telling you, Mijo," Terry smacked. "This strain we're working on for that new kombucha is gonna be a game-changer. At least that's the word. I don't even know what the fuck kombucha is. But you know what I do know? More sales for the client equals more money for us. And getting paid equals getting laid. Up top."

Terry held his hand out for a high five. When Miguel absently recip-
rocated, it felt like he was slapping a concrete wall. He hadn't been much
for conversation over the past thirty-six hours and change, and he must
have come off as particularly melancholy now.

"Say, any leads on Luis?" Terry asked.

"Nah," Miguel said.

"Huh?" Terry blurted, leaning in with his ridiculous, bandaged ears.

"No," Miguel repeated, just short of a yell. "Not yet."

"You know, I'm not saying the government had something to do with
it, but I'm not not saying that. Just my two cents."

"Yeah."

"Damn shame. But, hey, keep the faith, Mijo. We're on the man upstairs's time, not our own. Remember that."

The overhead LEDs washed the breakroom in a sterile pallor, and
Miguel caught himself drifting into a supernova of hot white, somewhere
far off. There was the craft, its geometry flawless, its movements exact.
Right. Up. Right. Up. Right. Up. There was Luis, the clearest vision of
him yet, his ivory coat brown-spotted and smooth, his ice cream-stained
muzzle yammering, legs bounding after the elusive night as if it were a
passing car tearing off into the distance. Or was he ascending? There was
also the woman in the window, and this was what Miguel could not get
over. This dummy of flesh preserved in terror or pleasure, or both. If
only she would remember what it was like to be animate.

"You ever forget who you are, Terry?" Miguel asked.

"Come again."

"You ever forget who you are?"

"Oh, all the time, man," Terry answered with great vigor. "Take this
morning: Woke up thinking I was William goddamn Wallace. You know,
the Braveheart guy? Was fit to throw on one of them flannel kilts and
start lopping off noggins."

"That's not really what I meant."

"Oh," Terry said.

"Do you think that all this, whatever this is, the light in the sky, everything that's happened since, is all about recapturing something that wasn't ever really there to begin with?"

Terry's face soured, and he became silent. His eyes went blank, like he was blacking out. Then, in a violent outburst that came from nowhere, he shot to his feet and flipped the foldout table across the room as Miguel remained seated, unsure of what to do or say. Not another word was spoken, another sound heard, save for Terry's disoriented panting.

A minute later, the shift supervisor poked his head into the room. "Christamighty," he said, investigating the scene. "Lay off the juice, will you, Terry?"

"I'm sorry, man," Terry said, his forehead and cheeks red with shame. "Sometimes it just feels like there's a buncha scorpions crammed into my skull. Little fire-colored fuckers scrambling shit up like eggs."

For a time after that, Miguel paced the parking lot across the street from the back of his apartment building. It was night again already. It always was. Balmy and close, the hour difficult to identify. These gaps in the rhythm of this reality were becoming more frequent, shapeshifting his constructs of truth. It wasn't just about the dog anymore; it was about these mountains, the texture of this sky, this little town, all its stupid mysteries, him. Miguel didn't know if he would ever get the answers he sought, and it was in that suffocating mausoleum of epiphany that the real horror was stowed.

As he made his way up the stairs to his apartment, Miguel heard those whimsical, cosmic synths that had become as familiar to him as a theme song. "You Are—I Am" fluttered through the same window at the historic hotel, sweet and clear. Miguel stopped and craned his neck to look into the room beyond, and what he saw was a stark naked man sprinting in circles around the walls, arms pumping, dick and balls flapping, mouth open as though he were screaming, but there was no screaming, or any other noise for that matter.

There was an obvious question Miguel wasn't speaking into existence:

Had it been aliens? There were explanations he found less plausible, sure. Man could not account for such numinous occurrences, such immaculate mechanisms. Nor could natural phenomena. There had to be something transcendent at the center of it all, something past understanding. Sitting there on his couch, stoned and watching television with the sound off, he suddenly recovered a memory. It wasn't complete, but it was important nonetheless.

Throughout his childhood, he had spent summers with his *abuela* on the outskirts of Guanajuato. Her neighbors raised pigs, and since Miguel struggled to make friends, the animals were his only companions—especially the piglets. One early evening as he played with Flaco, the runt of the bunch, a tremendous white flash ripped the fabric of the umber sky above the mountains to the west. A column of glaring light descended upon him, and before Miguel knew it, he was cast into an achromatic limbo. Whether it was for a millisecond or a year, he couldn't tell, but on the other side of it was an empty room made of glass, or maybe a material that didn't have a name. Miguel sat in the corner of it with Flaco in his arms, the piglet remarkably tranquil. He didn't see what approached him from the front, but he could hear it: a nonhuman strain of *rat-a-tat*, like windblown raindrops on tin, beautiful in its cadence. An unseen force tore Flaco from his clutches before he even had time to protest, and the animal was swallowed into the pale belly of nothing.

"Flaco!" Miguel called into the void after the piglet, but there wasn't so much as an echo. He wanted to cry, and yet a hidden power had muted his emotions, and his desire to follow was quickly quelled by the unknowable nature of the room, the contents of which lay whitewashed outside a radius of about five feet. Who had authored this blind laboratory of despair and uncertainty? Surely nothing Miguel had learned via his childhood faith or education, though he tried to locate it in one of those two categories. It was no use. Logic had no oxygen in a conscious nightmare.

The temporal dimensions of Miguel's human experience were torn at the seams, and the next thing he knew, he was back on Earth's surface, jogging in place as if bestride some treadmill that only he could see. He didn't realize it was morning until he forced himself still, a sensation of seasickness stirring its way into his guts. As his wits returned, he noticed something else, too: Flaco rested mere foot lengths away, recumbent and lifeless, weeping blood from the eyes and ears and mouth. Miguel nearly choked at the sight of him, and when he placed his small hand on the piglet's smooth rinds, it was like touching the surface of an ice cream freezer.

He couldn't even begin to imagine how he might have looked to his abuela, who sat on her couch clutching prayer beads as he stormed into her house, carrying on and making little to no sense.

"*¿Dónde estabas?*" she demanded, fraught with worry. She seized him by the shoulders. "*¡Miguel! ¿Dónde estabas?*"

Miguel found it hard to talk through the dry snag in his throat, and so he took his abuela by the wrist and hastened her outside to where Flaco's corpse had begun to settle in the clay. The piglet's eyes were black and open, cold, staring for an immeasurable distance at a sight perhaps reserved for Los Muertos.

"*¿Que pasó?*" Miguel's abuela asked.

"*No sé.*" He pointed at the sky, breaking blue and golden over the horizon. "*La luz. Era la luz.*"

His abuela looked at the piglet, then the sky, and then back at the piglet again. "*¡Es brujería!*"

Miguel had heard of strange things, dark things, superhuman things, emerging from the underground tunnels of Guanajuato City. The local kids had teased him about mummies and chupacabras and extraterrestrial *pitónes* of fire that roamed beneath the streets, but this was another matter. This was no scary bedside story. This was real, and he could only speculate as to the role the uncharted reaches of the universe played in it all.

He would grow up—and this he now remembered, too—to watch a documentary that Leslie Nielsen had narrated about the sea dandelion, or more specifically, the Dandelion Siphonophore, a colony of organisms assuming one, singular jellylike form. Bioluminescent orange-yellow with tubular pores, gracefully slender lappets, and acicular spines like one might find on an urchin. Most kept to the ocean floor, but occasionally, you could catch them stalking the open water with their gleaming gelatinous light like tiny torch bearers escorting souls to The Beyond.

Miguel had always figured aliens would look a lot like that.

Back on his couch, the phone rang. Terry. Miguel could practically smell the stink of the man's ears through the receiver, feel the oaf's raging, screaming pulse, begging to leap from its veins, as if it were his own, visualize his coworker straining and bearing down with a thousand convulsed muscles, shaking his monolithic head and uncaged tongue like a fucking animal gone rabid. Miguel sat on the other end of the line for several minutes, seeing it all in a continuous reel, never once saying hello.

Terry was a no-call, no-show at work for three straight days, each consisting of Miguel languishing through his duties, the shift supervisor pacing the floors of the plant, flummoxed by his employee's absence.

"Got me a mind to show up at that meathead's house," the bossman said on more than one occasion, to which Miguel shrugged his shoulders.

"Maybe you should call him again?"

"I'll call him, all right," said the supervisor, a confusing threat.

Miguel found that, though memories were coming back to him little by little, his grip on time was getting more and more tenuous. Had the Guanajuato Affair happened in this life or the one before? Had his abuela joined her ancestors last week or ten years ago? How long had Luis really been gone?

Regardless, Miguel doubted he would ever be reunited with his friend, and the simple thought of that made him ache. Made him feel lost, too.

He was at his mailbox, the leftmost slot at the top of the tenant cluster in the foyer of his apartment building, blinking, postured with his key drawn and extended before him. This is how things happened now: He was at Point A and then Point C with no Point B to bridge the two. Someone joined him from the right, a twentysomething woman digging through her purse at the opposite end of the receptacles. The name sticker above her slot read Dr. A. Carroll. Her sandy hair, streaked with veins of premature gray, was pulled into a messy bun, and heather scrubs hung loosely about her tall frame. Miguel didn't mind looking at her, but he also didn't want to make her uncomfortable, so he turned away. But then he was drawn back to her, the bizarre magnetism of familiarity that emanated from her.

"Do I know you?" he asked, somewhat regretting the question before he even finished. It sounded like a line.

"I don't think so," she said, avoiding eye contact.

"I'm Miguel."

"Andrea," she said out of the side of her face. She was having the worst time fishing for her mailbox key.

"Do you work at the hospital?"

"Yep. That's where I'm doing my residency."

She was being short, and there was a reason for it, but Miguel wasn't taking the hint. He was too distracted by the thought of Terry potentially being treated by this woman. Him sitting atop one of those medical exam chairs with the disposable paper covers, probably wearing a bro tank, her long fingers plugging his ears with cotton, her eyes widening at his abnormal testosterone levels. She still hadn't found her keys.

Finally, Miguel understood that his being there was only adding pressure. He made to leave when it clicked: "Wait. Weren't you in the storefront window?"

The question stilled her. "Excuse me?"

"The storefront window. Of the boutique next door. Were you... posing there with the mannequins one night recently?"

It was a ridiculous thing to ask. And he was sure of it, still. As she turned, revealing in full the features of her face, sharp-edged and long as if cut from limestone, he knew it had been her, rendered unmoving amongst the other effigies like she had dared to gaze into the headlights of some Gorgon creature. She shook her head no, eye whites welling clear.

"Pardon me for saying this, but it was you. I know it was."

Her mouth curled as though she were on the verge of smiling. Her nose went to bleeding. "I have no idea what you're talking about," she said.

Some time later, Miguel would doze on his couch. He would dream about his abuela, about Flaco, about Luis, all of them huddled together in that desolate, glasslike room aboard that innominate vessel, living in another dimension. If they were afraid, they weren't showing it, but he felt scared enough for the lot of them. The nonhuman voice was there, too, the one that had preceded Flaco's abduction, and this is what woke Miguel, left him befogged, slumped in the sitting room of his apartment with weed crumbs in his lap. Now, the light was pouring in.

Could it be that it was happening again?

He did not bother to open the blinds, but rather, decided to make directly for the landing out back instead. It was there, wasn't it? That terrific carapace, above the old mines to the north, drowning out the church and the house and the hedgerow and the stone wall. Lightning striking the same place twice. Manfred Mann was talking to him in that art rock way, and there was a finality to it, like something you know you'll be hearing for the last time. If there was at least closure, Miguel would be okay with it. In the end, all anybody really wants is answers.

His feet were on the sidewalk just outside of the parking lot, and the craft was overhead, its underbelly rotating counterclockwise so slowly it looked like an optical illusion. He couldn't tell if it was several miles away or right on top of him. As he reached for it, thinking he could touch it, there was a commotion behind him. A sudden sound, like a television that has gone from mute to high volume:

The naked man leaped through the window of his room in the historic hotel, hitting the ground hard and audibly breaking his legs. Possibly—likely—other bones, too. He gave no indication of pain, only propped himself on the heels of his hands and dragged himself along the building's back side like a dog that's been paralyzed from the hips down. Trying to get away from something. Or maybe going after it. Up the road, a silver Mitsubishi Diamante squealed forth into the night, hopped the parking lot curb, and before the damn thing could even come to a stop, out jumped Terry in nothing but his jockeys, looking like he had swum in a pool of blood, wielding one of those claymore sword replicas you might find at the flea market. One might say he had reached his final form, a butcher, a reincarnated barbarian turned loose on the imperial forces that sought to enslave him.

"I'll get 'em, Mijo!" the oaf cried, without any suggestion of who "them" actually was. He hollered "*Alba gu bràth*" with unadulterated madness in his eyes, and then commenced to slashing the absolute shit out of a random SUV. For all Miguel knew, that was the last thing his coworker ever did before he was hauled off to the boobie hatch.

Miguel knew he wouldn't be around to know how that storyline ended. Because it was happening. It had been this whole time.

The craft drifted across the building, toward the Main Street side, and as its antishadow kissed the ground, Miguel got the revelation he had been searching for. There, in the alley separating the boutique from a dissolved branch of the local bank, was Luis, his brown-spotted boy, so high-sheened in the brilliance you would think he had just come from the groomer, had been bathed in the cosmos. The dog stared at Miguel, ears folded forward, sad eyes a little squinty, leash in mouth, and maybe for an instant, just maybe, Miguel saw himself as a child, standing next to the animal, both of them doublewalkers wandered into the wrong corner of the galaxy. Then it was simply the dog again, wagging its sickle-shaped tail as it trotted deeper into the alley, away from its owner.

Miguel took off in pursuit. He shot down the narrow alley, rounded the corner. The woman, the doctor, stood in freeze-frame just inside the front window of the boutique again, and Miguel could feel her tumble over and wobble like a bowling pin as he passed. Ahead, Luis had broken into a hellacious gallop down Main Street, and the craft, though it didn't appear to be gaining speed overhead, was right on the dog's case. Miguel, trailing both his furry friend and the UFO, struggled to maintain a sufficient pace. He dug deep. Deep until his legs were numb and his lungs were empty. Deeper still until every single memory clawed its way out of his head. His abuela and Flaco, Terry and the other inhabitants of this strange, little mountain town, of the other strange places he had been, remembered and forgotten.

Out of Heaven floated a great Dandelion, breathing, warping through the air in the dog's direction like orange wax in a planet-sized lava lamp, and

Miguel knew fear, real fear, for the first time in his whole life. The scariest part wasn't the physical scene of what manifested ahead—it was the mystery of everything, catching up to him at once, bursting to get out. It was filling him up, stretching his skin to the brink. An ungodly brightness spilled out of him, and he was running, chasing Luis, hoping to get to him before the Dandelion did, and the dog was running, dragging his leash toward the blinding light.

March on Carthage

It came not as a thief in the night but as a mass extinction, more accelerated than anyone had imagined or predicted, culminating eastward, westward, north to south, over forests and deserts and plains and mountains and oceans, and not one was called to be in the sky but rather abandoned in a barren, sadistic Perdition born from the cruelest of dreams. A hellscape the world created to rid itself of the superficial filth.

It would've been quite something to have known her before the apocalypse arrived on Earth's doorstep.

Hannibal stared at her through his monster mask as he held his clasped hands toward the sky, low and gray and draped over them like a canopy. He exhaled slowly as she put a careful boot forward in the windswept wasteland, narrowing the distance between them.

She kept the silver steel of the .38 caliber handgun level with his throat because when she missed, she always missed high. He didn't look so sick, but she had been wrong before. She didn't want to do violence to him. But she would if she had to. She imagined she could do anything if she had to.

Hannibal loosened his fingers. As far as he knew, the town was otherwise forsaken—but he could never be sure. He had long ago come to terms with the likelihood of something stalking him in the heavy stillness. He hadn't had a choice. "I'm just passing through on my way to Carthage," he said with a thick and waxy voice. An old man's voice. "Please. I don't have any food." He nodded toward the canvas backpack in the sand sheet to his right. "See for yourself."

She mounted her thumb on the hammer. "There's nothing left in Carthage," she said, her words filtered through the respirator wrapped around her sun-stroked face.

He swallowed the stale air. "I'm going to visit my father. It's his birthday."

She glared at him as she circled left toward his backpack. "Don't bullshit me," she said. "I just told you. There's nobody there. You got any weapons?"

"Just a blade."

"Where?"

Hannibal titled his chin toward his collar. "Under my shirt."

She edged closer to him, keeping the gun aimed with her right hand as she extended the fingers of her left toward his fastened collar. She kept her eyes fixed on his as she undid the canvas shirt, button by button, until it parted. With surgeon steadiness, she removed the Ka-Bar fighting knife from its thermoplastic sheath, clipped at the hip to a strap that ran diagonally along his dried and blister-scarred torso.

She backed away and knelt beside the backpack. "You alone?" she asked as she began to rummage through his belongings.

Hannibal hesitated. "Yes."

"You're headed in the wrong direction, you know?" she said, combing through his blankets and spare garments. "All the salvageable land that's left on this continent is in Canada." She removed a legal pad and examined the writing within: blue and chewed and damn-near illegible. She held it toward him and shrugged.

"It's a calendar. I made it before—"

"You made this?"

He nodded.

She shook her head as she thumbed through the wrinkled pages. There must have been a dozen years to come within them. "This would be something else if time still existed," she said, looking at him to make sure he was still standing there with his eyes to the ground. She placed the gun next to her foot and scraped the bottom of his bag for anything she might have missed. Her hand emerged with a small brass trinket. She flipped it open. "A compass?"

"A gift."

She mulled over the current situation before grabbing the gun and rising to her feet. She approached slowly and studied his face, disguised by a vampiric Halloween getup that was poorly doctored with acrylic paint to convey blood spatter. "What's with that ridiculous mask?"

Hannibal began to grin, but he quickly suppressed it as if the world were normal again—a child in church with a funny thought in his head. "I guess it's supposed to ward off scavengers."

"How's that working for you?" she asked.

"Jury's still out."

"Take it off."

Hannibal removed his mask. He was just a kid—maybe twenty or twenty-one—lanky and awkward and baby-faced. The past year had found him wandering, sleepless and alone, a faded, chalky color surrounding the trenches beneath his eyes. And he was out there by himself, a knife his only salvation from unfathomable hells.

She took a step back, digesting the shaggy-haired sight before her eyes. She tucked the six-shooter into the front pocket of her tactical jacket before removing her hood and lowering her own mask.

Hannibal got a good look at her for the first time; he stared at her through a smoky trance as he swayed in the bitter heat. She had earthy brown eyes and a quicksand gaze that complemented her ruddy pallor. She was a good deal older than him, but the furrows of her face were beautifully sculpted—mapped out like roads leading to sunken cheekbones.

"What's your name?" she questioned, her voice deep and warm like nostalgia.

He cleared his throat. "Hannibal."

"I'm Olive."
"Like the tree?"
"Like the tree."

Hannibal and Olive navigated through the hollow heart of town, the air enveloping them acrid and dry. The ash-littered streets were lined on either side with cars charred beyond recognition, smoke still curling from some, and shards of glass lay jagged and sprinkled before gutted buildings like baleful mosaics. Soon the sky would redden and the night would come on, unforgiving over the permanent desert.

Hannibal kept pace at Olive's side as she minded him with a watchful eye. She had returned his bag, but only a few of its contents. "So what the hell are you doing this far in?" she asked.

He drew a sharp breath into his raw lungs. He didn't look well. "I was on my way to see my father when I ran out of supplies. I usually try to keep along the railroad, but I was desperate. I haven't had anything to eat in four days, and the last drink of water I had was almost twenty-four hours ago. I was gonna see what I could find here. I figured it'd be a better bet than the highway."

Olive ignored the first part of his statement and nodded as she briefly descended into her memories. She knew the highway; every once in a while she found herself there again in her mind amidst the clutter of abandoned cars and blackened bones cleaned of meat and tissue. She could hear the distant screams trapped in the fog of the horizon, bloodcurdling and lost. She could smell the undigested viscera that lay decomposed and strewn about for miles on end—the rotten fruits of human nature.

Hannibal mumbled as if weighing a decision.

Olive stirred herself from her morose reverie. "Do you know where we are?" she asked.

Hannibal's eyes gleamed at the question. "Loom City," he responded.

"How can you be sure?"

He pointed ahead. "The street markers. Oregon. Tennessee. Michigan.

Every street here's named after a state. Except for this one."

Olive looked up at the weathered green signs, the letters within them hardly discernible. He was right. She and Hannibal dragged along the main thoroughfare. Main Street dissected the town into two halves. The left-hand side was dressed with the remnants of small homes, their walls folded slightly inward toward their foundations. To the right, a vast, dilapidated brick edifice sat blanketed by a billowing wave of heat, the chain-link fence surrounding it warped and tarnished.

"The mill," Hannibal said.

"Anything in there?" Olive asked.

"Just scrap, far as I know. Metal *and* flesh."

Olive nodded toward a large, spire-crowned structure a quarter-mile further down the road. "What about there?"

Hannibal squinted at the belfry leaning atop it. "The Lutheran church. I'm sure they have a pantry, but it's probably tapped."

Olive looked into the sky, its dreary gray dwindling into dull vermillion as each minute became the next. The world was warmer than it had ever been, but there was still a chill to the air when the sun set. "Well, we don't have much of a choice," she said. "Besides, we need a place for the night."

Hannibal agreed, and they forged ahead. Caring for others wasn't characteristic of the life Olive currently knew. If she had stumbled upon anyone other than Hannibal, she very well may have buried a bullet between his eyes and backpedaled north until his corpse was a memory. But she had gone against her better judgment and decided to help him—if only until morning.

They had reached the church's adjacent parking lot when Olive stopped dead in her tracks. She lifted her index finger and pressed it against her mouth, shushing Hannibal as her eyes became wide and wild. A low jingle rattled through the dusky silence, and Hannibal's face washed clean with fear. Olive grabbed him, and they dove for refuge behind a pile of debris.

Moments later, a haggard figure shrouded in layers of indistinguishable material and soot pedaled sluggishly down the street as if leading an army of ghosts, the once-green bicycle beneath it overcome with rust.

As it drew closer, it began to hum a haunting tune, baritone and unnerving, a woeful spiritual out there in all that godless nothing. A wilderness prayer.

Hannibal peeked over the rubble and caught a glimpse of its face—stoic and stoned and grotesque like a gargoyle. It was an old woman. She stopped in the middle of the road before straddling her bicycle and burying both arms into the knapsack perched atop her handlebars. Her arms emerged with two heaping handfuls of a white, grainy substance. She didn't blink as she let it cascade over her fingers to the shriveled landscape below.

"What's she doing?" Hannibal whispered.

Olive offered no response. The old woman was unhinged, but she didn't appear physically ill. She balanced herself and began to cycle down the street in the opposite direction, crooning her forlorn song and ringing her bell. If Hannibal listened real close, he thought he could hear the marching behind her. Soon she disappeared into the evening haze, the small crystalline mounds in her wake the only proof that she hadn't been an apparition.

"What was that all about?" Hannibal asked, his breath erratic.

Olive stared at the bicycle tracks. "She was sowing the earth."

Dust drifted from the oak of the arched door as Olive pulled it open. The church's foyer was dim; the dying daylight from the world outside was the only illumination. Hannibal and Olive entered the sanctuary—blood-trimmed sky seeping through the stained-glass windows, revealing pews, overturned and gnarled. Hannibal and Olive waded through a graveyard of crumbled pages scattered about the center aisle. When they reached the altar, they looked to the wall behind the baptismal font and the yellow spray paint smeared across it.

It read:

On Vacation until further notice

They looked at each other.

Olive picked up a broken candle from the base of the pulpit and lit it with a long, thin matchstick that she pulled from the pocket of her tactical jacket. Hannibal followed as she led them down a narrow flight of stairs at the rear of the chancel, the air saturated with moldy aromas beneath dancing cobwebs. The basement kitchen was spacious; tin cans and plastic jugs lay empty along steel countertops. Olive opened the pantry only to find its shelves bare. Hannibal lifted the door of the icebox before letting it fall closed immediately.

Olive looked at his bleached face, noticing a putrid odor that she hadn't before. "Christ alive. What is that?"

Hannibal stepped back and grimaced at her through chapped lips. He turned and gagged, his eyes beginning to water as strings of saliva fell to his feet. He wiped his mouth with the back of his hand. "You don't wanna know."

They ascended the stairs into the sanctuary once more. Olive waved her candle about, searching the room. The starved light shone on a spiral staircase, suspended beside the organ in the corner. She climbed as Hannibal followed, and they found themselves in the pastor's study. The room, while malodorous and vacant, was in otherwise impeccable condition given the circumstances.

"Hold this," Olive said, handing the candle to Hannibal.

She heaved her duffle bag onto the floor in the center of the room; its thud surprised Hannibal, given the willowy frame of the woman who had been toting it. She removed a chair propped against a roll-top desk in the corner. Leveraging her weight against it, she broke off all of its legs and collected them. Then she underhanded them into the fireplace at the back, along with various papers she had gathered from the floor.

"Light," she said, reaching toward Hannibal.

He returned the candle to her. She lit one of the pages first and nurtured the fire, stirring the chair's legs and allowing them to catch. She returned to her bag as Hannibal caped himself with a blanket. He dropped to the floor and scooted in toward the warmth of the kindling flame.

Olive removed a canteen from her bag and drank sparingly. Then she tossed it to Hannibal, who turned it upside down and glutted with such eagerness that small runs began to stream from the corners of his mouth. He hadn't even asked to make sure it was boiled.

"Easy," Olive said.

"Sorry."

Next, Olive withdrew several cans from her bag, and Hannibal turned. His eyes grew cartoonish. She had food—and lots of it. Her bag was stockpiled with canned vegetables and pre-cooked meats. Hannibal's mouth began to water, hunger digging at his whimpering stomach like a dog, scooping its own festering wound with a flat, dry tongue.

Olive looked at him, and though she thought better of it, she couldn't circumvent the sheer desperation in his gaze. She slid a can of Spam across the floor in his direction and watched as he pounced on it like a fiend, his hands shaking as he peeled it open. He ripped the mask from his head and proceeded to devour the contents of the can as Olive removed her respirator and spread out her sleeping bag.

"You're not gonna eat?" Hannibal asked through a stuffed mouth.

"I ate earlier," she said, pulling her duffle bag under her head like a pillow.

Olive watched Hannibal as he finished his first meal in days. She didn't know why she had made an exception for him. Maybe it was the innocence. Maybe it was the loneliness. Maybe it was the stupid, makeshift trick-or-trick mask. Maybe he projected an energy she had known to be extinct. Maybe he was good.

"You don't belong out here, you know?" Olive said.

"How do you figure?" Hannibal asked, swallowing the last of his dinner.

"You don't belong out here with these barbarous men. They're animals."

"You mean the zombies?"

"They're not zombies. Zombies die first. These people are very much alive. They've just been pushed to the brink, is all. Point is, you don't belong in the same space."

"I do okay," Hannibal said, his eyes spellbound by the fire.

"So, what were you doing traveling south?"

Hannibal frowned. "I told you," he said. "I'm going to see my father. In Carthage."

"It's his birthday, right?" Olive questioned. The sarcasm in her tone went over Hannibal's head.

"Tomorrow," he responded.

"How do you—" Olive began to question before remembering that she had confiscated his homemade calendar earlier in the day. She altered her course. "How do you know he's still there?"

He locked onto her with unchanging eyes. "I know."

Thunder rolled on the other side of the wall as the fire inside began to crackle, its harsh, scorching notes pervading the room.

"Why doesn't time exist?" Hannibal asked.

Olive's face curled in confusion. "What?"

"Earlier. You made a remark that time doesn't exist. What makes you say that?"

They sat there in silence for a moment as Olive looked into the fire. "Before everything was gone." She paused. "Before everything was gone, not long after the permafrost out west melted and the TSE spread eastward, my husband and I were living with a camp of people on the state line. It was no paradise by any means, but we made do. We were going to gradually make our way up to the border. That was the plan, at least. Then my husband was one of the first ones to get sick. It was slower than I'd expected. General confusion and exhaustion at first, like he was just dehydrated. And the cough. Loss of taste and smell. The agitation didn't come for almost a week. He started having these terrible fits of mania, emotional extremes. Everyone told me to kill him. Said I had to. I wouldn't, so we were exiled.

"We were on the road for maybe two days when he came for me. Wrapped his hands around my neck while I slept. So I reached into my bag for my thirty-eight, put the barrel on his chin, and pulled the trigger. Covered myself with his blood. He didn't make a sound. He staggered at first, but then he just laid down to the flat of his back. He just laid there and died, this human animal so broken and pitiful. He accepted it—the inevitability of it. Some sense of clarity in all the rotten shit that had infiltrated his brain. He hadn't stopped looking at me the whole time. And in a way, I'm not sure he ever will." She looked at Hannibal. "That's when I knew that it was only a matter of time. And time isn't relevant. It's all for nothing." She paused again. "I mean, we're the generation that gets to see the world end. What kind of dumb luck is that?"

Hannibal fiddled his fingers. It was obvious that he didn't know what to say.

Olive sighed before changing the subject. "Where were *you* coming from?"

"Just outside Richmond."

She looked at him in astonishment. "You came all the way from Richmond with nothing but some clothes and a compass to wish your dad a happy birthday?" She was still humoring him as far as she was concerned. "That's over two-hundred miles."

Hannibal removed the compass from his pocket, its face speckled with dirt and years. "I'd barely started grade school when he gave me this. He told me no matter where I was or how bad things got, as long as I had this I'd always be able to find my way home. Every October sixth since I was born, I've spent with my father. He's eleven miles away. I can be there by dusk."

Olive nodded. For the first time she believed him. She shook the heaviness from her eyelids as she propped her head against her bag.

Hannibal looked at the compass. "Think I could have my knife back, too?"

"Don't push it," she said. "Get some sleep. I'll take the first watch."

It was sometime just before dawn when Hannibal awoke to a winding croak of sound—a special effect suitable for a haunted house. The alarm set in as soon as he opened his eyes: He had fucked up and fallen asleep on his watch. He glanced around in the firelight, but his new companion was nowhere to be found.

"Olive?"

Only the shadows responded.

He sat up and began to entertain the idea that she had deserted him.

Then something shifted in the darkness to his left.

"Olive?" Hannibal repeated. "Is that you?"

Nothing again.

Hannibal tried to stand. From the right, an unseeable force floored him once more. There was a brief struggle, fingers raking over Hannibal's forehead and nose. As soon as he was able to pry them off, he made out an affectless face dimmed by the sparse lighting. It belonged to the old woman who had been sowing the earth.

"Get off me," Hannibal ordered, surprised by her strength.

Her expression was vacuous, but the madness was all over her. Maybe not in its final stages, but it was well on its way. She tugged at Hannibal's ears, tried to claw his eyes.

"Get the fuck off!"

"The city is sacked," the old woman growled. "Don't you see? The city is *sacked*. Let it be. Let it *die*. Die with me."

She opened her maw of decaying teeth as if posturing to cough on him. That's when the tip of Hannibal's knife shot through her mouth, and the woman's face locked into a freeze-frame of fleeting life. Thick globules of blood ran down the length of the blade and dripped onto Hannibal's chest. She keeled over onto the floor next to him.

Olive stepped forward into the light and planted a boot into the old woman's back. She removed the knife with both hands, a shrieking noise echoing into the room as the steel slid through bone. "Are you all right?" she asked Hannibal.

He exhaled. "Yeah."

"We better get going."

Hannibal and Olive made their way to the edge of town, the train tracks along it laced over the swollen earth. The coming day cast a murky fog over everything, making it difficult to discern where the earth ended and where the sky began. But, like the day before, the couple welcomed the reprieve from the sun—no matter how temporary it might have been.

Hannibal yawned unsatisfying sleep from his heavy chest, still shaken by the incident in the church. But he couldn't afford to dwell on it. Neither of them could. No good would come of such inclinations in this age of expired reason. His mind turned elsewhere. "What do you miss most?" he asked.

"What?"

"You know," Hannibal said. "What do you miss from before?"

Olive sighed in vexation as she put one foot in front of the other through the low visibility of the morning. "It's too early for questions."

Hannibal tucked his chin like a child scolded in school for talking in class.

The silence that followed fell over Olive like shame, and she was surprised at how guilty it left her. For the first time in her life, she couldn't remember being anything but bitter. She looked upward at the drab sky, hovering above them like a pall.

"The beach," she said.

"The beach?"

"The beach. It's where we lived. It's under water now, of course. I miss the stars there, burning in the night like a million candles never extinguished. Watching over the children of God, good and bad." Olive stopped walking. "The smell of the ocean and sunscreen. The grittiness of the sand on our tile floors. My Lettera thirty-two. My dogs. Being moved to laugh, to cry, to anything." She looked at Hannibal, who had stopped with her. "What about you?"

Hannibal paused. "It wasn't really a thing, I guess. It was a sound. A whistle." He closed his eyes. "The whistle at quitting time. My father worked second shift at the mill in Loom City, and sometimes, when I was little, if I'd saved up enough money, I'd ride the bus out to meet him at shift change." He laughed. "Damn thing rang out like a banshee with steam breath. Some people found it shrill and unpleasant, but to me, it always felt like home. My father would be beat up pretty good. He'd be covered in grease and oil, and he'd be dead tired, but when I ran up to him, he'd lift me off my feet, just like we were at the beach and the water was getting too deep."

Olive stared at Hannibal as if she longed for his memory.

He opened his eyes. "There's been times since everything happened that I've thought of that whistle—imagined it."

"When was the last time?" Olive asked.

"I didn't leave Richmond without food. I stumbled across a group of scavengers somewhere around Norlina. Nasty-looking guys, but they weren't sick. Shanks and kitchen knives and baseball bats with nails hammered through them. They told me I was lucky they were so nice. Said if it'd been anyone else, I'd be with the Lord. After they took the food, one of them suggested I take my knife and bleed myself out. Said he'd pray for me."

Olive gulped. "My God."

"It could've been worse," Hannibal said. "They could've ate me. Lord knows I've heard of such. Or they could've just killed me and left me for someone else, I guess." He looked into Olive's eyes for more than a moment. Like he had found something new in them. "But then I wouldn't have made a new friend."

Olive looked back at him, and a strange feeling came over her. His story had touched her like nothing had in a long time. He reminded her of someone she'd known in college—the mannerisms and the modesty and the boyish handsomeness. And suddenly she realized she couldn't remember the last time she had made love.

He leaned in close. "Can I ask you something?"

"Yes."

"What kind of dogs did you have?"

Olive sighed. "Weimaraners," she said.

Hannibal smiled and began to walk forward again.

Olive shook her head and watched as he trotted ahead, rawboned and far too punchdrunk for someone his age. And all at once, a profound warmth etched cracks into the bitterness.

"You coming?" Hannibal asked from ahead.

By noon, Hannibal and Olive were walking more closely than they had before, kicking rocks through the subsiding fog and ever-present smoke as they headed southwest toward Carthage.

"How do you even know where your father is?" Olive asked. "Isn't everything gone?"

Hannibal grinned. "Main Street runs into Route two thirty-nine, and we're the first house a quarter-mile down the road. Been in the family for generations. It's got a scrolled balcony that we used to watch the sunset from, and a veranda underneath with rocking chairs and swings. I used to go there when my nerves got the best of me. There's a lawn out front where me and my father used to play catch. You can't miss it."

"And you're sure he's still there?" Olive asked.

She had no more than finished her question when a hawk soared overhead, dust dripping from its pinions as it departed north. Its massive wings stretched, broad and robust, as it glided almost celestially through the grim sky. Hannibal and Olive continued to gaze upward, long after it had vanished. Then the sun came out.

"Maybe it ain't all for nothing after all," Hannibal said.

Maybe it wasn't.

Olive continued to walk ahead. "Isn't it funny?" she asked.

"Isn't what funny?"

"Isn't it funny how we found each other in the middle, in a place where the streets are all named after states?" She smiled for the first time.

Hannibal smiled back through his mask. They were five miles from the city limits, and plenty of day remained. He opened his compass and thought of his father. Hannibal had a lot to tell him. Tears began to well in his eyes as the needle confirmed his direction.

A mile later, they came upon a building that was in uncommonly good shape.

"The Olde Carthage Train Station," Hannibal remarked, though he didn't need to say anything; the platform was a dead giveaway.

"Suppose it's worth a look?"

"Probably wouldn't hurt."

Hannibal lent Olive a hand over the platform, and they entered the lusterless building. There were no departures, no arrivals. Benches were upended, and whispers of activity remained, but there was nothing worth salvaging there.

Nothing material, at least.

Olive approached Hannibal from behind, her heart racing, and she could tell he knew she was there. He turned around and stared at her intently. He took her neck in his hand, and despite the danger lurking at every corner around them, they kissed. She swept her fingers along his leg and grabbed him, feeling his body, his size, feeling the shape of him. He removed her jacket and shirt with a deliberate hunger, his open palms sliding down the small of her back. He moved his hand into her pants. And then he touched her. She couldn't remember the last time that had happened, but she had missed it. She had missed it so much.

They fucked slowly on the floor, but he came fast, and she wasn't far behind. She was surprised at how much she could enjoy it in all this turmoil. After, they held each other for an indeterminable amount of time, enjoying each other's skin, enjoying the body heat. The last two people on Earth.

Hannibal and Olive left the train station maybe an hour after they had arrived. The sun was now beating down on the arid land with a renewed fury. They took a break to share Olive's canteen, somewhat regretting the energy they had expelled, but not too much, and pushed onward for a few miles closer to Carthage. Hannibal began to let up with each step, an unpleasant tingling sensation spreading through his body. The wears of the road.

"Keep up," Olive called as she continued ahead.

"Hold on," he replied, kneeling to tighten his boot. Olive kept walking. Hannibal began to pull at his frayed laces when he heard a snapping sound to his right. He rose to his feet. Cautiously, and against his better instincts, he approached the emaciated tree-line at the fringe of the tracks, a foul odor permeating his nostrils with every step he took. It was rotten in the way that only flesh can be rotten. His heart began to palpitate as he pulled back a stiff branch and looked at an uprooted tree just ahead.

The human carcass lay disemboweled at the base of the naked tree, a hulking man—broad and well over six feet in height—crouched directly above it, body matter cupped in his hands as he leered at Hannibal through cloudy eyes. He rose to his feet, licking his bloody lips, his gore-bedewed bomber jacket shining above his prey. He stepped over the body and began to snarl behind the leather skin of his face, worn like an old baseball glove. Sickness full-blown.

Hannibal took a step back and clenched his fists. He flinched once before taking off toward the railroad, retracing the same direction he had come from. The man charged after him, blood-drunk and barking like a hound as wet flesh flew from his jaws. Hannibal tripped over his own feet just before the tracks as the man chasing him lunged forward; they fell to the ground together.

"Olive!" Hannibal screamed in fear.

The man pinned Hannibal against the railroad bank, strands of entrails and sinew dangling from his chin, eyebrows arched. Specks of carnage peppered Hannibal's face as he struggled beneath. His peripheral vision caught sight of Olive darting toward him in the distance. He reached to his hip in despair, only to find his knife missing. The man continued to hold Hannibal down with his left hand as he delivered a devastating blow with his right. Then the man reached to the ground next to him. He lifted his hand above Hannibal's chest once more, this time clutching a railroad spike. Hannibal grabbed the man's wrist in an attempt to hold him off, but he wasn't strong enough. The spike entered next to Hannibal's sternum slowly and deeply as he retched. The man removed it and hovered above Hannibal briefly before a sequence of pops rang out into the air, sending bullwhips of blood to the parched earth. The man collapsed to the ground.

Olive dove to Hannibal's side. "No," she cried. "No, no, no." She cradled Hannibal's head and touched his gushing wound with her trembling hands, but she didn't know where to start. Hannibal looked into her eyes, blood pouring from his mouth. When they had met, he had felt her cold, but the last thing he felt was her radiating warmth as she laid his head in her lap and his gray eyes fell lifeless.

Olive reached the city limits just before dusk. Downtown Carthage was a skeleton comprised of brick and mortar bones. She had taken Main Street to Route 239 just as Hannibal had said, the imminent night brooding on the horizon. The first house on the right was once white; its cupolas were now reposed, stained deep and leaden.

Olive sauntered down the front lawn walkway toward the porch. She entered the house to find it like so many others she had encountered on her travels: desolate and bleak. She checked all the rooms, her steps echoing throughout walls and hallways like a haint. Swinging the storm door open, she exited through the back of the house and found herself in what had once likely been a lush pasture.

She walked for a while forward before she stopped. She closed her eyes, and she finally understood. She took one more step forward before heaving her bag to the ground and sitting in the dead, brittle crabgrass beneath her.

She struggled to find words. She struggled to remember if Hannibal had really been there or not. "Your son was the type of person that—" she paused. "I'm sorry. I'm not good at this type of thing. Your son was the type of person that you felt like you knew your whole life when you'd only just met them. Too often people muddy things up by saying things they don't know, or saying things that just aren't true. So, I'm just going to say what I know. I know that your son did the best he could against impossible odds. I know that he kept on breathing." She choked up. "I know that he loved you. But above all, I know that he was brave. And I know that he was good. He was just the boy among wolves in the pale blood of night."

Olive removed the compass from the pocket of her parka and placed it on the smooth headstone in front of her. She looped her arms through the straps of her bag, dust falling from her shoulders as she departed north into the darkness.

Copperheads

What if they told you the Word had it turned around: that God was the snake, and the Devil, the creator?

The fog lazed over the countryside like a sunning animal, smoke-thick and the color of a blue jay, the beasts of the new morning retreating behind it on either side of the rut-shot road, things you could feel but not see, like shame. The Reverend Mackey Feaster maneuvered the truck blindly along, at times with only his knees, the grille chewing breathy horseflies, the old, deaf Rhodesian Ridgeback panting the gray rot of its gums into the cab through the sliding rear window, and little Jack Thomasin in the passenger seat counting all the hidden objects of the wilderness.

"Preacher. How can you even see where you're steering this thing?"

"Cain't you?"

"Nosir. I cain't see nothing."

"That's because we're all blind, boy. Difference is the Lord is my eyes. You gotta let Him be yours, too. Gotta let Him be your mouth and your nose and ears. Listen to what He's telling you at all times."

"What's He telling me now?"

Sweat oily and beading across the splintered windshield, the ride was a blurry waking dream, a feverish thing from inside the head of a drunk: Feaster cranked his window down, inviting the outside among them, and it accepted the gesture like a sinner receiving grace, the strange incoming wind of it swallowed by the Ridgeback's nostrils and spat out through the dog's maw, invisible, and if you could drown in the air, Jack reckoned it would be a lot like this.

Something of a smile on the reverend's face.

"You feel that warmth? That bubbling *ka-thump-a-thump*? Like the Master's holding a match to the earth? Means He's cooking up something real good. Means He's fixing to move. They'll be ripe today, yessir. Mark my words."

One after another they came in desperate, sinuous lines, bending around that trailer deep into Mudcat Holler like an impossible tail, and with them various gifts reflective of their means: baked goods and homemade bread baskets and knockoff French soaps and fresh herbs or else rolling tobacco. Wandering the unknown, their souls inside-out masks. The seer sat upon an antique chair in front of the hide-a-bed, pulling on the cigarette through its slender holder, looking very much like a woman dragged in from the previous century, crinkled butcher paper skin sagging over bones, eyes flush, milky as silverbells, and there were patchouli candles, not for light but rather to ward off unwelcome auras.

Jack Thomasin's bit in all this was to accept the good-faith offerings and remain otherwise mouthless, tucked into the shadows while his grandmother remarked on the fates in that throaty voice that never sounded like it could quite get clear. What's the chances the mill is hiring come winter and will sickness befall me and which lotto numbers should I choose and is my husband running around on me all over creation? The answers were almost never what anybody wanted to hear, and that's what gave them such endless credibility.

Then, through the beaded curtain proceeded an attractive, empty-handed feller in a brownhide suit jacket and stiff dungarees, and with him a dull, stagnant heat like the aftertaste of lightning, and Jack closed his eyes and made himself go to someplace that wasn't Glass, North

Carolina. There were mountains and seas and skies and all the other things the universe sends to let you know that you might not be nothing, but you're close.

With the boy and the dog flanking either side of him, Feaster bounced over the wet farmland as if it were a pulpit, wooden crate in his hands. Yes, Lord, he would make a big production out of it every Sunday at what used to be the fire station, shooting down that sliding pole, running in place like he didn't have feet, shouting the Gospel at his flock, and them carrying on, bucking and flopping and screaming in their suffocating fish dance. Nothing was known of the good reverend's origins, but he was handsome in the way of old Hollywood movie stars, and when he had lifted that cancer right out of Miss Cassie's body whilst guest-spotting one Wednesday night service, folks reckoned they ought not question the work of God, whose mysterious ways was His business, not theirs.

The dog now stalked ahead, and Jack kicked along through the emerging dankness, counting the knuckles in the Ridgeback's spine while he dwelled on the day before, in the darkened single-wide. Feaster's hunting eyes jumped from point to point on the ground with a cadence that didn't seem normal for a thing animated by warm blood, and the mere existence of them left the boy cold.

"What're we doing out here?"

"Why, the honest, soul-warshing work of the Lord. That's what."

"Okay. Whose land is this?"

"Don't matter. This is God's land, son."

A hurst of gum trees pitched upward before a feeble crick ahead, and this bizarre search party made for it like a traveling band of nomads, the Ridgeback out front and unaffected by a tandem of thick-haunched squirrels darting across the buffalograss. The morning was talking; you just had to listen. Embedded into the rest of the vegetation was a lone olive tree that had no earthly business in Glass, North Carolina, its branches curled outward in mostly fruitless spiders.

"Well, would you look at that. 'But I am like a green olive tree in the house of God: I trust in the mercy of God forever and ever.'"

A single drupe dangled in front of the reverend, shriveled and bilic yellow like a sick liver, and he plucked the fruit from its silvery mother and placed it upon his tongue and closed his mouth. The flavor of it, which Jack could only speculate to be overripe and foul, contorted the reverend's face into a rictus of indescribable pleasure. In but a moment, Feaster's attention turned toward the trickle of the watercourse a stone's throw downwind of their current position, the dog already lumbering that way. Remembering why they had come.

With breath as sour as bad wine: "That's where they'll be, over yonder. They like it down there."

"Who's they?"

"You'll know when you see them."

The crick was paralleled by a collection of neglected woodpiles like so many bonfires never started, and Feaster sent the boy after the ones the Ridgeback passed while he scouted the other direction. Jack combed the damp stacks, clueless of what he was looking for, as the dog sniffed and milled about, mindlessly eating grass and making stupid sounds from its snout. They had gone a good piece when he heard it, this crackling noise that was half rustle, half whisper, and when Jack set his eyes upon the waterside of the closest woodpile, not five feet away, his stomach rolled.

There in the dirt reeled a writhing pit of hourglasses, tan and pink and brown, leaking air. It was always this way, the earth breathing in drum beats, Jack just hadn't noticed it until now. He counted four heads in the den by their delicate, forked tongues, the bodies too wound up to understand their true length and broadness. He made to call for the reverend, but Feaster was already there, standing over the boy's shoulder, still and intoxicated with some unknowable emotion. Mouth glistening with olive juice.

"See the way they move, O child of God. The Holy Ghost itself is a moving thing, always working, never resting, churning the fat of your heart."

"Preacher, I'm scared."

"You should be. That's the divine agency of Conviction, weighing down on you. It ain't gonna stop 'til every knee bows and every tongue confesses."

There was something quietly violent, lewd, even, about the way the snakes conducted their revolutions, hissing and slinking over one another, thick and tired. But then they fell hushed and motionless, and perhaps Jack found this most impressive of all, their ability to assume the appearance of nothing, this mass of silent hostility, waiting to do that act which nature had reserved for it.

"Will you pray?"

Jack's hair stood on end, and he sank to the ground, facing the pit, tears already sloping his jawbone before he even knew they had started. How could vipers exist in such a way, as anything other than solitary creatures? Were they juveniles or adults? All the boy knew is they reminded him of death.

"'Behold, I give unto you power to tread on serpents and scorpions, and over all the power of the enemy: and nothing shall by any means hurt you...'"

Jack felt the words mealy in his mouth, but before he could recite them, the Ridgeback stepped forward from the boy's periphery, whining at first but then reporting growls through its throat, head dipped, ropey neck muscles bulging, forepaws trembling energy. Feaster was content to let this play out, the dog establishing itself as a barrier between the boy and the den of snakes in a biblical standoff. To the reverend, it may have been a sin to intervene. Just as well, little materialized over the next several breaths until, as if answering some higher calling, a single snake lifted its rusty head an inch above the greater jumble. The Ridgeback chomped, but it was much too slow on the draw, the reptile snapping forward and sinking its fangs into the dog's meaty flank before a blink could come and go. Another one sprang forth, and then another.

"It's a beautiful day the Lord has made."

"Then why have you brung malice into my home?"

"I come on behalf of the boy."

"Perhaps you come on behalf of yourself. Does the reverend request a prognostication?"

"I don't need one. Them that have accepted the Blood already know what the future holds, the peace which passeth all understanding. Maybe if you'd put away all this witchcraft and false prophetry and crack open a Bible, if you even own one, you'd understand that. Naw, I come in the name of intercession for that child. On special business for the Lord. You've brung judgment upon yourself, but there ain't no reason to involve him."

Mackey Feaster was by no means a big man, and yet, in this moment, he appeared as though the room might not hold him, his head close to fracturing the ceiling and propelling him toward Rapture high above Mudcat Holler, above Glass, North Carolina, above the reticulating landscape of the wicked world. The surrounding dimness gave things the impression of floating, and Jack, perched upon a foot stool in the corner, perceived nothing below him, felt only an inward tightening as he was pulled in opposite directions like a finger trap, and there were unspoken cries for mercy that went unanswered. If the boy unseated himself, there was no telling where he would wind up.

Smoke had a way of finding everything, and Jack sometimes wondered if that was all his maw maw could imagine. Smoke. Great screens of it etched into the film of her eyes, shapes and colors and textures leaping into the light of her mind like river trout. The seer projected an air of boredom and indifference, but the boy knew this was not the case.

"Jack, do you wanna go with the reverend?"

"I don't know."

"If you're what you say you are, why don't you tell us how he'll choose?"

"You understand nothing."

"I understand you're a fraud. This is a hellbound enterprise you're running. With your gimmickry and your voodoos. You orta be ashamed of yourself, leading them astray, them poor people lined up out there. They might not can see through it, but you ain't fooling me. The blood'll be on your hands."

Jack pictured his maw maw cupping her knobby fingers into a sieve through which red water dripped to the floor in dull pings, constant as clock strokes, as time itself, and you could imagine it, couldn't you, the rhythm of it, if you tried hard enough?

"If that's all, Reverend, I think it's best you leave. There's people requiring help this day."

"That we can agree on. I'll be back in the morning, Jack. Providence has laid an important mission on my heart. Think about whether or not you wanna be on the right side of eternity."

The reverend was gone with nothing to show for the penumbra he had occupied, and with his departure, the seer lit another cigarette, fixed a shawl over her shoulders, though it was not cold. Jack scooted his stool closer to where his maw maw sat, within the cocoon of her spent smoke. He liked to think she could see him, the features of his face, the expressions, but she just stared right through him, looked through everything she touched with her eyes as if it were a ghost, and maybe everything was. Maybe there was a secret about the universe that only she knew.

"Maw Maw. How do I know what to believe?"

"Believe what you can see, darling."

"But you cain't see."

"You couldn't be more wrong."

The dog staggered off elsewhere to lie in the grass and lick at its wounds, three or four of them, and the snakes retreated into the nest, communicating amongst themselves with their skin. Jack's vision had briefly dissociated from his eyeballs, but he was coming back, realizing he had stood to his feet, his loud heart forging a sword of terror in his chest that made swallowing unthinkable. The reverend had not budged, had not seemed pained by his four-legged companion's distress.

"Be still, and know that I am God."

"Yessir."

Feaster placed the crate on the ground and crept forward a boot-length, the words on his lips turning less human by the syllable until they were sharp, woody rasps, what the old-timers might refer to as tongues. A flicker of white heat could not cut the sky so thin. The snakes wheeled aggravated as ever, but only one among them appeared posed to answer another perceived threat, its arrowhead primed by some invisible bowstring. What vanity a man must possess to take its language as his own, to show up on the doorstep of its house unannounced.

"You ain't trying to catch it, are you? Don't you need one of them sticks with the hook on it to catch a snake?"

"I only need that which the Master giveth me."

The reverend readied his hands as an open basketball player might, preparing them for the catch, and Jack had never seen someone sweat so much in his entire life. There was a flash of forever, and then it happened so fast, the postured viper quickening, pulling its body taut, teeth finding purchase just below the knot on Feaster's outer wrist, and him grunting, cussing, pinching the devil by its neck with his free hand. The reverend jerked the snake away from its brothers and sisters, and it was pissed, its tail coiling and unfurling in protest as its captor subdued it in the air and then wrangled it into the crate, out of breath. He lidded the makeshift cage like the stony tomb of Christ, and it was finished for now.

"Hallelujah, yessiree."

"Are you all right, Preacher?"

Two holes, equidistant to one another, oozed scarlet over the flesh of the reverend's arm, and he onced over them, unimpressed.

"Aw, that ain't nothing but a little scratch, boy. Barely broke the skin."

Feaster took hold of the crate, stiffened up, and looking upon the rest of the snakes, which had for whatever reason decided against aggression, headed back for the truck joyously. Jack committed each of these creatures to memory, a conflicted sympathy welling in his heart, and he knew that there was not a shred of conscience among them, but still he hurt. The Ridgeback limped after its master with its tail tucked, in a bad way, and Jack came along as well, drew even with Feaster as the morning reached its fullness, the brim of it overflowing with blue pain.

"Do you know why they call 'em copperheads?"

"Because they're the color of copper?"

"Well. To a simple-minded feller, yes. But a spiritual man knows better, amen. Copperheads serve as a conductor between the power of the Lord and his children. Yessir, that power flows like a current, like a big ol' wave of the Holy Spirit through everyone who will but have it, and only then is the land ready for redemption."

I had a vision last night. Everything was dancing and throwing itself at fire, passing through to the other side like some black magic miracle, and the music was a pipe organ, echoey, but not no hymn I've ever heard before, and I've heard them all. We stood barefoot beneath exotic trees that had been struck, on smooth banks of clay that sang cooly between our toes, sent shivers up our legs and into our backbones; we were thankful. Heaven was empty. And I seen great winding rivers of blood, revealing themselves in dramatic, spiraling gesticulations that ended at some point, but we couldn't see where. Would you be baptized in them? Let them put out the fire even if they, in doing so, filled up the balloons of your lungs until you were breathless and drowned? A liar was riding on the back of an immense crawler through the water, and one by one we sank to the bottom, and we were blind save for our clumsy red faith.

The Praise Team was swelled up with the Good News, listing side to side there in front of a set of lockers that had never been removed from the wall, clapping and singing, letting the sweet Spirit run out of them like serum from a poked blister, and the congregation, twenty or so, cheering them on, high on the dope of salvation. At the firehouse church, early service was the only service. More often than not, they would spend the whole Sabbath there, hollering and weeping and cutting a rug and laying hands. Something was coming, yes; Jack had sensed it all the way on his bike ride, when the morning had not yet let go of the night.

One of the members was a carpenter by trade, and he had fashioned a workable altar out of some imported balsa wood from the hardware store. A distended shape rested atop it now, enshrouded by an off-white bedsheet, and it was calmly reeking, but nobody was ready to talk about that. Here came the Reverend Mackey Feaster, descending the stairwell this time rather than the sliding pole, and would you believe, he had that damn crate with him, hugged to his chest, the wrist of the hand that had been bit hidden from view. Jack knew sorrow by the way it concealed itself from the light.

Feaster looked far from well, clammy and pallid with flu or else some kind of psychological affliction. Yet he grinned at the Praise Team, offering his obligatory amens and hallelujahs and all listens. As soon as the last song was finished, the reverend shifted his focus toward his congregation, gathered throughout the large room in the same folding chairs the alcoholics used on Monday nights. Man, woman, and child stared back at their interceder, eager for the message, the poems of guilt and forgiveness, the portraits of kingdoms and wastelands.

"You know, last week, after service, I was thinking about how good God is."

"That's right."

"To give us a roof to worship under, to give us voices to cry out with. To burden our hearts with conviction."

"Amen. Yessir."

"And how do we repay Him for all He's done? We get lazy and complacent. We get comfortable in His house while everything outside of it goes down the commode one day at a time. We don't go to God no more. We wait for God to come to us, to those who's lost. Friends, it don't work that way."

"Right."

Tallow never shined like the reverend did now, white that was begging for blue, and his breaths were performative in their labored mechanisms. There was a madness in his eyes that didn't have a name. Jack understood that it was too late.

"What we've created here together is good, don't get me wrong. But what untold miracles we could accomplish if we would but accept the blessings of God that's out there for the picking. What we need, what this country needs, is a old-fashioned, Holy Ghost revival. But it ain't just gonna happen. We gotta plant that seed, light that fuse, however you wanna say it. We gotta take the gifts of God's Promise and put them to use."

"How, Preacher?"

"With Old Time Religion. The kind of them folks out in Tennessee and Kentucky and Ohio-way."

Feaster sat the crate on the floor; he was looking at Jack, he was looking at everybody. It was then the boy noticed the reverend's wrist, purple and necrosed, given to tremendous swelling. Feaster ripped the sheet from the altar, and there were gasps and moans at the sight of the planked Rhodesian Ridgeback, stiff and bloated, festering puncture wounds gone septic. Feaster was seamless with his turn toward the crate, crouching, lifting the lid, and tossing it to the side, reaching in with reckless arrogance. He hoisted the copperhead end-to-end above the dog's corpse like a handler at a carnival as sinners stood, shaking, high-stepping, moving ferally.

"'And these signs shall follow them that believe; In my name shall they cast out devils; they shall speak with new tongues. They shall take up serpents; and if they drink any deadly thing, it shall not hurt them; they shall lay hands on the sick, and they shall recover...'

"Friends, I've been to Hell and back! I been around poisoning the earth like salt. There's been cocaine in this nose and creekwater in this belly, and I've been in whorehouses from here to Timbuktu. I have two-stepped with the fallen angels, and I've been on the verge of Death itself! It was the belief that brought me back from the mouth of the beast, belief! that can bring back those forgotten souls in the highways and in the hedges, bring you back..."

Rise, boy! Rise! Rise in the name of God Almighty. The dog moved. Everything around you broke like the ocean, and no one was saved from it. Was it divine intervention? Was it only your eyes showing you what you wanted to see? You saw the handsome reverend, watched him heave sweat glittering, stinking, into the natural light. The copper-head opened its mouth, showed you its fangs, and if they pulled the nails out of the hands of Christ, the feet, they might look something like that. Your Maw Maw, the seer of Mudcat Holler, got her sight back because she had never lost it, and you are Jack Thomasin, child of God, you are Jack Thomasin, genuflecting, sobbing, born...

And you believe you believe you believe.

I was not offended

I

1944. Twins born in an outhouse in a place called Beechum. The boy named Justice, the girl Selene. An aurora of green parachuting above the birth pain spiritual. Babies thrust into a curious world without their consent. The father dead in a mill accident, the mother a laundromat hand.

Something else in the gloaming, coyote hymns. Fragrance of afterbirth. The segregated part of town. Out here, magic travels by the blued train tracks. Out here, the Devil dances like lightning.

Justice is the earth, and Selene is the fire. Wild children, barefoot, alive by night. Their beautiful skin luminous like oil. The boy's biology is a helix of mischief. Where he goes, the sister follows. The white part of town in the earliest years, the gin joints in their own neck of the woods later on. Justice worships the Blues players there: Shaky Wilburn, Boomerang George Stinson, Clarette Joseph, Storm Palmer. Gods of the space between.

Late in the day, summer '53:

Selene pedals, restless on her side of the straw mattress. Sighs like a tired breeze. She wants acknowledgment from her brother. He doesn't oblige.

"Mama asleep yet?" she whispers into the dark. "I cain't hear her snoring."

"She ain't even been laid down for five minutes," Justice says. "Scooch over."

"Where we going tonight? The Redgum or Pluto's?"

"*We* ain't going nowhere. Your backside is staying in this bed. Now keep on your side, dammit."

"We'll see about that."

Mama should have named his sister Trouble, Justice thinks. She is headstrong, saucy, too smart for her own damn good. Annoying, like the piece of skin that hangs from the roof of a burnt mouth. Younger by seconds that feel like years. Persistent.

If there's one thing Justice has on her, it's patience. He waits 'til her chest begins to labor with the deep breath of sleep. Focuses real hard on the room, shut of light like a starless outer space. The minute he hears Mama singing her snoring song, he shimmies out of the covers and steps his long john-covered legs through his only pair of trousers. He rakes his hands over the top of his head, taming the close hair, then high steps for the window. Almost inches it open, too, when he hears the rustling behind him.

"You ain't slick," Selene says, and Justice can feel the resentment to his teeth.

"Go back to bed."

"No. Where we going?"

"Go back to bed!" he repeats, nearly breaking whisper.

"Be a real shame if Mama was to make you pick out a switch again," Selene tisks.

The gall.

157

"All right," Justice concedes, lifting the window the rest of the way open. "Come on."

Under the cover of night. The siblings shadow the curvature of the railroad's body. Beechum's crooked spine. Pluto's is a mile or so down the holler, next to the crick. A make-do lumber cabin with a slanted tin roof, front porch railing like a bottom row of snaggy teeth, some missing. A cast, not quite violet, inseparable from smoke. The language within is a heartbeat through cotton: music, laughter, boozy nothings committed to the night and then left there forever.

Justice wants so desperately to speak it. To be old enough to understand it.

The twins slip unnoticed through the backdoor. The joint is wall to wall with folks dancing, sweating, being, drinking. A dog in the corner that could be a hundred different breeds. Everything is blue monochrome and shines. Sticky, woebegone rhythms clog the air, a muddy-smooth voice behind them. Somewhere in the muck, there is hurt.

Storm Palmer's spider-leg fingers don't match his fat frame, but the way they contort around the fretboard of a guitar makes him the best there is. He dresses nice, has a thin mustache and a conk hairstyle like they wear in the city. He fidgets in his chair like a schoolchild while he's playing. He bleeds you slow:

"Shot my brother down, south of Injun Head,
Traded his whiskey drink for a bellyful of lead.
Said they shot my brother down, south of Injun Head,
Traded his whiskey drink for a bellyful of lead.
I been up and down the Atlantic Coast,
From Dover to Darien.
But I swear on my mama's grave,
I ain't going back to Maryland."

Through Justice's body, chills.

There's a whine. Hard to tell if it's coming from the crowd or the kneaded strings of the instrument. The bridge. Storm Palmer simmers to a conclusion. Sweat blisters his cheeks. Patrons lay their adoration on thick, and the Blues Lord walks his guitar to a single table in the corner.

"I'm gonna go talk to him," Selene says.

"No, you ain't," Justice says. He reaches for his sister's arm, but she is already gone. He whispers a word he thinks is a curse, waits a beat and a half before he goes looking for her. Ducks through the labyrinth of hot bodies 'til he is right behind her.

Storm Palmer is bent forward, closing the latches on his guitar case. He paws for a lowball glass of clear liquid on the table next to him, and that is when he notices the twins. He produces an oystery, sigmoid-shaped smile that is difficult to put a read on.

"What're y'all doing here?"

No answer.

"A little late for youngins to be on the loose, especially at a place such as this."

"Just come to listen to the music," Selene says.

The Blues player's mirthful laugh is a radiator hiss: "Y'all like the musicians, do you?"

"Yessir."

"Who's your favorite?"

"Clarette Joseph. She sings real pretty."

Storm Palmer nods. "Well, you're in luck because she's on next. Of course, I reckon I should be telling y'all to run along. But I can keep a secret if you can."

Selene's mouth curls, her eyebrows jump in elation.

"What about you, little man? You got a favorite?"

"You," Justice says, sheepish.

"My boy," Storm Palmer says. "Gimme some skin."

Justice does, and he can almost feel the electricity from the Blues player's fingertips.

"You ever play at The Easy?" Selene asks.

"Naw, gal. That's in the white part of town."

As Storm Palmer says this, Justice catches sight of an impossibly tall, pale-skinned figure at the other side of the room. Gangster suit, gangster shoes. A man, Justice thinks. Selene sees it, too. It stops and turns, just enough to notice. It flashes the children a beaconlike wink, ducks through a beaded curtain. Nobody else gives the impression that they have seen it.

"How come white folks can come here, but we cain't go there?" Selene asks.

Storm Palmer looks at his brogan shoes, then back up. "Now that's a matter for a different hour, young lady. You just remember that the Blues is the language of black folks. Don't you let nobody tell you different."

"Yessir," the twins say.

The Blues Lord takes a drink.

Elsewhere, a stirring. Dozens of conversations taper off like departing footfalls; the floorboards cease their squeaking. Even the Craps players at the back have paused their game.

Storm Palmer smiles. "Here you go, gal."

Justice thinks Clarette Joseph is the most beautiful woman he has ever laid eyes on. A queen. Something he has been told time and again that his people cannot be. Every eye in the building is on her sapphire wiggle dress, which hugs her shapely body like a cast. She has a face that says more with expressions than most people can with words. She holds every ear in the building by a thread.

Selene bounces on the balls of her feet, hands pressed together like a madonna.

Clarette Joseph steps up to the mic, wets her lips. She hums at first, a gracile-looking man whom Justice recognizes as Boomerang George Stinson on the piano behind her. Her croons beget words after the instrumental intro:

> "Every time I think of home,
> There's a rhythm in the trees,
> A windy summer song,
> And it brings me to my knees.
> I'm going home,
> Where don't nobody know my name."

Her sound is a silky contralto with near-perfect pitch control. Rising easy on the wings of the keys and then falling through the air in downy barbs. There is sadness, but there is also sweetness. It makes you ache. She is well into the chorus when Justice realizes that his sister is singing along with her. The little girl sways in place. Every syllable a mirror.

Clarette Joseph sees it, too. She smiles so big it looks like it hurts. Breaks from the song: "Go on, child."

"Me?" Selene mouths in disbelief.

The singer shakes her head yes. "Why don't you come sing with me, darling?"

Selene is slack-jawed, a state Justice has never seen her in. She approaches her idol in a dizzied stride. Barely comes up past Clarette Joseph's hips. Most of the patrons go along with it. Some of them clap.

"From the top, Boom," Clarette Joseph says. Her hand a vine on the girl's shoulder.

The pianist plays the intro again.

They sing:

> "Every time I think of home,
> There's a rhythm in the trees,
> A windy summer song,
> And it brings me to my knees."

Clarette Joseph trails off. Leaves the girl to continue solo. Eyes closed, Selene belts it out:

> "I'm going home,

Where don't nobody know my name.
Since I hitched that ride from Slab Town,
Things ain't never been the same."

Justice is shaken. His sister has a voice. The type that a nine-year-old should not have. Like it was stolen. The type that latches on to the pit of your stomach and doesn't let go. It is raw and unlearned, but it is nonetheless powerful, rangy, convicting. Clarette Joseph claps along and laughs. Pluto's finest are duly impressed. Justice feels something else. It backbuilds, a supercell squall line looking to hit the same area twice. Envy.

When Selene finishes her last note, she is met with standing whistles and hollers. The kind that not even the regular performers get. Clarette Joseph crouches down to say something to her.

Storm Palmer shakes his head at Justice. "I don't know, son," he says. "Might not be too long before your sister is out here with us every night."

The jealousy stings, and Justice's only defense is to turn away from the scene. He finds himself looking toward the beaded curtain across the room. The tall, pale-skinned person is there behind it. Then they are not.

Selene won't shut up.
The whole next day:
Did you hear 'em?
Did you see their faces?
Mister Storm said I was a natural.
Miz Clarette said she couldn't sing like that when she was little.

If Justice lets her know it bothers him, she wins. That's what being siblings is all about: winners and losers.

After supper, Justice sneaks out of the house while his sister is washing up for bed. There is a field across the neighborhood that is sawgrass and wildflowers. Beyond that, the railroad. The boy comes here every now and then to work through his problems, despite the obvious dangers. Copperheads, train hoppers, broken glass, and other debris. Rumors

162

of necromancy. They say you can see your reflection in the train tracks, but he never does.

The camel crickets underfoot know the boy's melancholy. They console him with their lonesome cadence. The night is a visitor, and it brings a friend with it. From the bend of his eye, Justice picks up on the incoming silhouette. Shifty long with postlike limbs and an ill-fitting white suit, a pork pie hat. A case strapped along its back. Not at all your typical hitcher. It dances so fluid. It is one place, and then it is another. It is close enough for Justice to see.

"Evening," the voice says, a man.

The figure from Pluto's. At this distance, he is almost wooden, the exposed parts of his body not quite skin, but rather a milky plaster. He grins. In the trace of his lips, dozens of scores. As if his mouth has just been ripped open after a century of being sewn shut.

The boy tries to remember how to run, but he can't. He can't remember a lot of things.

"Haven't I seen you before?" the man asks.

"You were at Pluto's last night," Justice stutters.

"Right you are," the man says, waving a finger. Something drops from his sleeve and into the grass. A maggot. "And what business does a young fella like you have out there?"

Not a word.

"Come on, now. I won't bite."

"Wanted to see Storm Palmer."

The man smooths out the lapels of his suit, does a little number with his feet. "Can't say I blame you for that. Boy's gotta have his heroes, and Storm's one of the greats."

Justice can't get over how tall the stranger is. The boy thinks he could stand on his sister's shoulders and still not see the man eye to eye. If he has eyes. Everything above the nostrils is shaded by the brim of the hat. Everything about him is dodgy and reeks of carrion. Yet Justice is drawn into him like a keeper to a horseshoe magnet.

"What if I was to tell you that you could be better than Storm Palmer ever dreamed of being?" the man asks. "What would you have to say about that?"

"I'd think you just got out of the boobie hatch."

The man blurts a laugh, the caw of a crow. Reels it back in as if he had temporarily forgotten his place. "You're all right, kid," he says.

"Why're you asking me all these questions?"

"Bear with me," the man says. He unshoulders the case from his back, opens it. The moon catches the sheep-gut strings of a gorgeous black guitar.

"Whoa," Justice hears himself saying aloud.

"Why don't you take it for a spin?"

Justice squats down and almost touches it. At last, a moment of hesitance. "What's your name?" he asks.

"It's not important," the man says. "Folks around here have called me all manner of things over the years."

"I cain't trust nobody won't tell me their name."

"Good boy," the man concedes. "Okay, call me Smiley."

"Smiley?"

"Smiley." The man twists his slitted lips into another grin.

Justice lifts the guitar out of its case, a glossy obsidian artifact that looks brand new but feels real old. He is stilled by reverence.

"Go on, now," Smiley urges. "Pick that thing, my boy. I know you've seen how it's done."

Justice strums at the strings, clueless. At first, his fingers fumble along the instrument, but then a miracle: The flats and misses give way to a coherent melody. In no time, his hands fly up and down the fretboard with remarkable dexterity. Making unthinkable sounds, animal sounds. Movements of a virtuoso. Blues mixed with genres that don't even exist yet. His face wears the mark of disbelief, his eyes of a welcome betrayal.

"Fun, ain't it?" Smiley says.

"How am I doing this?"

Smiley snaps his fingers, and like that, the boy loses his bearings. His hypnotic licks run clumsy, drunk. Painful to the ears. He is the same boy who has never picked up a guitar before. Selene's lesser brother.

Smiley toes the ground. "You wanna be able to play like that all the time? You wanna be a star?"

Justice tells him yes.

"Not everyone is born with talent. Sometimes, you gotta take it."

"How?" Justice asks.

The stranger smiles a smile, a centipede with broke legs.

"Bad people wait 'til dark to do their laundry," an old Blues player once said. Justice can think about nothing else the night after his visit from Smiley. Blood bubbling down the ridges of a washboard, a thick lather. Cloth wringing out smothered screams from drowned lungs. A tin tub baptism in reverse.

Sometimes, you gotta take it.

"What're we waiting for?" Selene asks. "Mama's out cold."

"Just another minute," Justice says.

Funny thing, time. In the nine years they have shared this small bedroom, suffered each other's oddities, time hasn't seemed to matter at all. But now it does, and Justice wishes he had more of it. He can't concern himself with it *and* keep his wits. He shoves it aside, thinks of his sister singing. How it made him seethe with resentment.

They depart the house later than usual. The grass is slick from a suppertime shower. On Selene's mind is Pluto's, on Justice's, something else. Tonight, there are no constellations. Tonight, only a benthic sweep of sky harboring untold species of secrets. Scrub. Rinse. Dip. Ring. Repeat.

"You think Miz Clarette will be there?" Selene asks, kicking a spray of stray ballast onto the train tracks.

"Beats me," Justice says.

"What about Mister Storm?"

"I don't know, Selene."

"Why do you sound so blue?"

"I ain't."

Justice knows right from wrong as a matter of simple arithmetic. He sees the superficial numbers and what they equal beyond the moment: One bad deed, like the one he has in his heart, does not negate what could be. Yet he grapples with it. There is time to change his mind 'til there isn't.

A yoke of pale light dots the horizon ahead, doubles in size. There is a percussion of metal against itself. A wrought-iron rhythm, monophonic, not unlike a song of tremendous sorrow. And then the vocals, a blunt blast of air that starts and ends the same. A colossus telling you that it's coming, that there is nothing you can do to stop it.

"Train coming, Juss," Selene announces from a little ahead.

The boy knows. The graveyard freighter on a northward run. Its smokebox expiring a crest of exhaust, its grated pilot like the mouth of a large steel annelid crawling forward. The girl plugs her ears with her fingers as she watches it with wonderment. Everything is new and breathes.

Now close enough to wake the hair on necks, arms, legs. The horn makes its loudest report. Justice can feel the blood in his veins cooking, the wholes of his eyes like silver dollars snaring sunlight. Selene glances back. She looks so small. In the years to come, her brother will think about many things. Sitting next to each other during the more serious parts of church, trying not to laugh. Stealing air-dried tobacco leaves from Mr. Hobie's barn, chewing them and getting stomach sick together. Feeding the sheep and goats at the Hallman farm. Foot races along these same train tracks, their shapes stretched skinny across the ties.

But he does not think about any of that now.

Justice grabs his twin sister by the shoulders. He slings her to the tracks before he can lose his belly. She doesn't scream as she falls. She doesn't scream as the juggernaut barrels over her, or if she does, it is lost in the roaring. All else is lost there, too. The dismemberment of her body. The innocence of childhood. The stillness of night. Blood shed so violent.

One car inseparable from the next. Justice observes as the freighter carries on, the longest he has ever seen. At some point during the procession, a weight on his shoulder. The boy doesn't even have to look up to know that it is Smiley's hand. From the cufflink, a ripe maggot twitches onto Justice's collarbone.

II

Four years like the white seeds of a dandelion in spring's breath. There and then not. Justice in the ultramarine glow of Pluto's. It is 1957, and he is thirteen years old. When patrons aren't looking, he steals skims of backwash hard liquor from their glasses. When they are looking, they see him with sympathy in their eyes. A still-grieving brother never made whole. They do not know his crime.

The music that plays in the background now is as much a part of Justice as anything else. He does not exist outside of it. Many nights he has let it pour out of him into the dark. Nobody to talk to but the silence. Now in the gin joint, same as it ever was, the boy inspects the guitar, horizontal in his lap. It is not nice. He had to work months of odd jobs to afford it. But it makes noise, the only requisite.

Between acts, a familiar face.

"Hey, Mister Storm."

The Blues Lord looks up from the guitar he's wiping. "Howboutya, little man?" he says, like he recognizes Justice but doesn't at the same time.

"You on next?"

"You know it."

"I'd like to play with you."

"With me?" Storm Palmer says, bemused. "Right now?"

"Yessir."

"I'm—I'm sorry, son, but I'm more of a fly solo type of cat."

Justice cocks his head like someone has called his name, faces away, and Storm Palmer's memory kicks in.

"You're the boy, ain't you?" the Blues player says. He doesn't even have to say the rest.

Justice nods that he is.

"Can you play?"

Justice nods that he can.

"All right, let's see what you can do."

The audience takes a turn for the silent as the duo is seated. The seasoned musician, the too-small-for-his-britches boy. Justice tunes his instrument, hears throats clear, chairs slide on the floor.

"Any requests?" Storm Palmer asks his new partner.

"I wanna play that song about how they shot your brother."

"'Maryland'?" the Blues player says, taken aback. "I ain't played that song in about—"

"Four years," Justice finishes. "Do you remember it?"

"You bet."

Storm Palmer counts it off, and the pair begins to strum. They play the rhythm together, the elder bobbing his head in surprised approval. The boy's style, smooth and natural. He makes quick work of winning over the crowd, now swaying and nodding. A feel-good moment.

They go into the chorus, the second verse. Out of the second chorus, a revelation. Justice breaks into an impromptu bottleneck guitar solo. With eyes closed, the boy bends the strings into transcendent textures of sound: a creature at the end of its life cycle, a human machine, a tempest being conceived, an angel having a conversation with a demon. It is Delta Blues with a hard twist; it is breathtaking hellish agony. A horrific mastery of physics.

Storm Palmer is so baffled that he has forgotten how to play. The others so rapt they can't take their eyes off Justice. They witness a generational talent being born right in front of them. They do not witness what Justice is witnessing beneath the music. The train dragging the child's body a quarter-mile or so down the track before the pieces begin to disperse. The blood-slicked rails deep with light. Men wrestling remains away from coyotes and buzzards like table scraps, shooing them off with sticks. A mother's cry so alien that it feels as though it was put into her body by an outside force.

There is the presence of something else in the room. Something that cannot be seen or heard per se. A synesthesia of the occult. Popping up through the gathered like snapshots. Everybody has a different name for it. For Justice, it's Smiley.

The boy concludes his solo with a flourish of improvised finger-picking along the highest frets. The last string plucked, he opens his eyes, awakening from a dream. Half the audience puts their hands together for him, half can only stare, mystified. It is the first time something has turned for Justice. An object in his mind like a pleasurable parasite. It doesn't bother him one bit.

They will play together for many years, these two. Justice Caldwell and Huddie "Storm" Palmer. Five or six nights a week. From Justice's youth into his young manhood. They will play the gospel- and folk-driven classics; they will play the jump and swing backbeats of the new originals. The younger learning from the elder, but mostly a beneficiary of a blood contract.

The landscape around them changing, wet clay in the hands of God. So is Justice. No longer small but rather lean and leggy, narrow-chested. Overalls traded for a hand-me-down herringbone suit. Pompadour hair-do, a mouth that is never missing a hand-rolled cigarette.

An evening that could just as well be any other. Justice perfect and clean on the six-string, Storm Palmer lilting the lyrics to "Hellhound on My Trail," the Johnson masterwork. The duo puts on a fine rendition—so fine that the Blues Lord is compelled to recite the final verse three times. The last word perishing into a gulf of smoke and easy vibes, Justice's fingers take on a life of their own. Those digits riff into sound-scapes that no longer resemble Blues but rather a novel genre. Groovy, unkempt, nonlinear. A bastard Rock 'n Roll. Electric turns on acoustic hardware. Voltaic larva in an underground circuit.

Many listeners squinch with satisfaction as the solo builds. Some gaze, skeptical. Among the latter is Storm Palmer. Something troubled in the Blues Lord's eyes. A fixed expression like he doesn't understand, like he fears what he is hearing or doesn't trust it. Like he knows his pupil has outgrown him, that their paths will now diverge.

Justice performs with a breakneck fever that brings him to his knees. A desperate prayer. If he doesn't release the rhythm in his head, it might destroy him. *She* might destroy him. He doesn't know how she got there, but she is all the same. A naughty creepy-crawly feasting on decaying matter. The music leaches from the boy, now a man, like poison.

This is Justice's purge, and he will carry it with him from here. Some men his age will go to Vietnam, others out west. Justice will go to Clarksville, then Louisville, then Joliet. The places in between. The bars and the clubs. Justice will go to Detroit.

III

Backstage at some venue, Justice in the dressing room mirror. A galactic leap between here and Beechum. Another time, another space. Picture the young man:

Babyface, thin strip of facial hair on the chin. Orange cavalier hat with lightning blue feather, orange drawstring cape with canary yellow boa quills. Silk blouse to match the color of the feather, unbuttoned to the navel. Liquor and grass in his blood, a little bit of LSD. He has retired his old archtop in favor of an electric Strat, which he now twiddles at with both of his wiry hands. A practice number. It is always Storm Palmer's "Maryland."

A restless energy on the other side of this wall. Writhing. Blood blister relieved by a cutting voice: "From the Motor City, please give a round of applause for Wormbrain."

Justice moves toward the blue. The music hall is the sound of a hundred passing cars, obscure beyond the stage lights. An auditorium afire with hunger, begging for scraps. And Justice will feed them. He comes to the microphone, a stagehand plugging his guitar into an amplifier to the side. He scratches the strings, wordless, threading the needle of a melody that is as technical as it is hallucinatory.

The supporting instruments collide. This is Wormbrain's first headlining tour, but they have already earned a significant reputation by word of mouth. Justice has a band behind him. A rhythm guitarist, a bassist, a drummer, someone who plays the keyboard and various horns. But it is all about him. His Blues-soaked vocals, his jazzy freestyle guitar playing. Far-out lyrics. Comets shooting through space. Wolves hunting for dinner. God as a young child. Sororicide.

Justice's rise has been meteoric. Part of him knows his fall will be the same way, but he does not dwell on that when he's out here. When he's on this stage, he is overtaken by a blur of perception. An orgasm of sound and color. From time to time, he even forgets the lyrics to his own songs, yet he continues to saw away at that guitar like it is just him in that field where he first met Smiley. Paled by moonlight.

On one such occasion during this particular show, Wormbrain is well into its set. A four-minute guitar solo has turned twelve-minute production thanks to an off-the-cuff Justice guitar solo. Ropes of sweat fling from his face as he whirls like a spinning top, cape a house flag in a high wind. He is so engulfed by the gale that he is late to notice how hot his strumming hand has become. He steals a glance at his burning fingers, winces when he notices that sparks are flying from the strings. Actual sparks. But he can't stop, can't pull his hand out of the incinerator. The audience cheers as though these pyrotechnics are part of the act.

A few trips up and down the neck later, Justice's guitar bursts into flames. He wraps up the solo with a heavy *wah-wah* effect and spikes the instrument onto the floor in front of him. A member of the stage crew rushes out with a fire extinguisher, and Justice makes an early exit right—much to the surprise of his bandmates. There is unrest throughout the auditorium, the kind of chaos that Justice thrives on. The gratification of it teems at his nerve endings. It is practically crawling atop his skin.

It is *actually* crawling atop his skin.

He peers down to discover a maggot, fat and wet, corkscrewing the index finger of his playing hand. "Shit," he gasps, brushing it off. He shakes like some wild thing come out of the water as he steps beyond the curtain into the dressing room.

"Annoying, ain't they?" The words are misty cool, sugary.

There is an old chaise lounge fit for a Turkish smoking room in the corner, an obscure figure occupying it. This figure rises, comes toward the light. The girl is in tatters. Tears in her homemade full-skirted swing dress and stockings, exposing graying, hide-like skin, a jerky gouge in her crimsoned collar. An arm, a leg, held together at the elbow and knee respectively by stringy tendons. She is missing an eye, and where the flesh of a cheek should be below that empty socket, there are only naked gums and teeth. The whole of her rippling with frantic motion. This, Justice quickly learns, is because she is covered head to toe in maggots.

"Try having a million of them," Selene says.

There is no singular emotion that strikes Justice, but nausea is the strongest. He must devote all of his energy toward making sure he doesn't vomit.

"What's the matter?" she says, closing the distance. An ineffable stench. She talks older, even though she doesn't look it. Her parasite-ridden skin squeaks. "Ain't got no love for your sister?"

Justice chokes it out: "I seen them lower that box into the ground myself. You ain't supposed to be alive."

"Don't worry, brother. I'm not."

A maggot, plumper and longer than the rest, a maggot overlord, slips through the girl's open cheek and into her vacant eye socket.

Justice feels like he should sit, but he can't. "Then how are you here? Why?"

"On behalf of a mutual friend."

Justice knows who, but won't dare speak his name.

"I just wanna know, was it worth it?" Selene says, inhaling the dressing room. "Even as you're standing here right now, I can tell you think it was."

"No."

"You ain't gotta lie to me; I'm your blood. How else would you have got all this? Little boy from the wrong side of the tracks in a place like Beechum. You did what you had to do."

Her brother swats at his earlobe, where something is wriggling. Another maggot smacks the floor. Justice props himself against the back of a chair, tongue-tied.

Selene wheels back toward the dressing room mirror, unbothered by the gruesome reflection she finds there. "Too good to talk to me?" she asks, a sibling's teasing tone. "You may have all these white folks fooled into thinking you're some kind of rockstar, but you're just the same old Justice to me. Couldn't carry a tune in a bucket. Come out the same mud as me, will go back into it."

Justice has been able to keep everything at a distance, only calling upon that night when performing. The defense mechanics of the mind have shielded him from confronting it head-on. But now it has all come rushing back. It is squirming. It is rotting. It is fetid.

"What do you want?" he asks.

"Ain't about what I want," his sister says. "It's about what you owe. It's about the fine print, so to speak."

"I cain't take it back."

"Ain't asking you to."

One by one, maggots begin to appear from the hidden creases of Justice's clothes, his body. He can't slap them away fast enough. "Call them off," he whines. "Ain't gotta be like this."

"You made a deal, Juss," Selene says. "You had to know it was only a matter of time before you became like this."

"Call them off, Selene. Please."

"Sometimes you gotta take it. Sound familiar?"

"Call them off!"

"Well, sometimes it'll come back to take *you*."

Justice starts to dancing like he had seen church folk do as a boy. He is flailing, kicking, jumping, running in place. The room is the world beyond a mad carousel. All a smear. He is shrinking, and he is festering, and he cannot tell what is maggot and what is fabric and what is skin. He is a spiral. He begins to wonder if this is how he will die, and if it is, he hopes it will happen faster than he deserves.

Then a voice, not Selene's: "Justice."

Justice is suddenly liberated from his conniption. There are no more maggots. There is no Selene. It is only he and Wormbrain's drummer, Graydog.

"You all right, man?"

"Yeah," he responds. "Yeah, I'm good. I've gotta take it easy on the acid, Gray."

Behind Justice, a slowly closing door. Turning on its hinges. Keeping whatever is inside of it. Keeping it like secrets.

At the tour's next stop, Justice debuts a song. The lights lowered to mealy shades of red and purple. The composition bluesier, more somber than anything he has written in a long time:

"Looking at the moon from the cellar window,
My heart's an open sore, her blood is a memento.
Have you ever heard of a night so cruel and strange?
Mama cried her name, but I couldn't steal the pain.
There's some things in this life that you cain't never change.
Yes, there's some things in this life that you cain't never change.
The caravan screamed, and the coyote howled."

He plays it through a headful of diamonds, blinding the synapses. His elaborate, reverb-heavy riffs build cathedrals of sound in the air. His eager congregation will follow him to the end of this Earth and back. If they have to. Somewhere among them is Selene. Justice cannot see her, but he can smell her. He can also smell a different scent, equally miasmic. One he hasn't picked up in years.

Was it worth it?

Justice is shitfaced when the photographer shows up. A pretty girl named Tina. Wormbrain has made the cover of a well-known pop culture magazine, and she is to shoot the frontman solo at a local gallery.

"Your sound is so unique," Tina says. In her outward appearance, Justice detects a former J-school student with suburban roots who hasn't fully committed to this lifestyle yet. "Rock, Blues, Jazz, Psychedelia. I don't think I've ever heard anything like it."

Justice smiles, his head too swimmy to respond like he should. He is wearing a colorful Egyptian tunic with a mink stole, a handful of rings, courtesy of the record label.

"Do you mind me asking how you came up with it?" Tina questions.

There is the shudder of a Blues Lord, a white man, a maggot girl, a bug made of boxcars in his conscience. "Don't really know," he says.

"I very much doubt that," she says, and she is close. So close that Justice can feel the heat from her body. She leans in, but rather than touching him, inserts a joint between her lips. She lights it, takes a drag. Offers it to him, he accepts.

The studio is dim save for the lights over the exhibits. Tina directs Justice toward a pop art mural of a clown-faced woman in dominatrix leather eating a yellow pear. He slumps against it as the photographer tells him what persona to adopt, her camera shuttering.

You don't care about anything and you're on your deathbed and you're thinking about a girl you want to fuck.

They pass the joint back and forth. If only those poor folks in Beechum could see him now. Those fools with their dirt and their hardscrabble, sun-up-to-sun-down lives, and their empty pockets. Hard lines dug into their faces like shallow graves. Difficult to say they would approve of the black magic by which he came into this life. But they are there, and he is here. He will live with that.

In the next exhibit, a headless lion has been felled by a sword-wielding Christ. Braids of snakes sprout from the open neck and plait at the feet of the messiah. There is a deep stained glass effect, and it carves crushes of ice into Tina's irises. Justice is shameless in his appraisal of them, and it makes Tina blush.

"What's the headline?" Justice asks, striking a pose.

"I'm sorry?"

"The headline on the cover. Do you know?"

"'Tasting the Mind of the Universe,'" Tina says, raising the viewfinder to her eye.

"I like it."

"The editor said it's from a quote of yours."

"Sounds about right."

She snaps the camera. "What does it mean?"

"Can mean a lot of things," Justice slurs.

"Like what?"

"Can I show you?"

Tina draws into him, and he strokes her neck just beneath the jawline. Fingers her necklace. There is a creatural air about him, the same one that feeds into his guitar-playing, feeds like a pup on its mother's kill. It is this, too, that makes him charming, irresistible in the eyes of anything he wants—no matter how little he did to earn it.

"Let me see your hands," Tina whispers.

Justice raises his right, and Tina takes it in both of hers. She traces the lines of the palm, the grooves of the knuckles, kisses the fingertips.

"How long do we have this place?" Justice asks.

"All day," she says, dropping to her knees.

After, on the floor. Justice sobering by the minute, Tina playing with his curly chest hair. A mutual understanding that this will be the extent of their relationship, and so they are enjoying it while they can.

"This isn't the first time something like this has happened for you, I take it," Tina says.

"Naw," Justice admits. "It's not. First time with someone like you, though."

She laughs. "Someone like me?"

"Most of the people that follow or write about our music are hippies, deadbeats, bohemians. I don't pin you as any of those."

Tina looks off into the darkness of the gallery. "I'm not ready to go for broke on this yet. I love Rock 'n Roll, don't get me wrong, but I also want to go to Heaven. I come from a place where the two are mutually exclusive."

Justice is quiet for a minute, and then he says, "I don't believe in Heaven. Well, I hope it don't exist, at least."

"And why do you say that?"

"Because if it does, I won't be there."

Sleep finds Justice a short time later. He dreams of Tina in a field of sawgrass and wildflowers, awash with moonshine, showing her back to him. He is again a boy from the squalor, barefoot. The camel crickets sing a work song while he labors toward her through the thick. As Tina turns, maggots burst from the pores of her skin like cheese through a grater. But it is not Tina at all. It is Selene.

Behind her, a freighter lumbers past. On one of the boxcars, the mural of the clown-faced dominatrix eating the yellow pear. The boy tries to scream, but his little voice is a coyote cry.

When Justice thrashes to consciousness on the floor of the studio, Tina is nowhere to be found. Nor is his sister. He is naked and alone. But something remains. In the painting above him, it is no longer Christ who holds the sword above the decapitated lion. It is Smiley.

The tour blurring on, night after night, each show leaving something behind like a carcass. After a while, Justice no longer knows which city he is in, and it doesn't matter anyway. The maggots come more frequent now, hatching from his scalp, his collar and shirt cuff, his pant leg. They are stirring some kind of production within him. A concert, a feast. He will not know fully until it happens.

"Tasting the Mind of the Universe" has hit newsstands across the nation, roped in new fans to the mystique of this burgeoning talent who might hold the future of music in his gifted hands. And so Justice finds himself behind a blue curtain, the kind of blue that had painted every corner of Pluto's, gazing out into a sold-out theater.

Do they know what he did?

During the sound check, an unprovoked sensation sets into his right eye. It is twitching and burrowing. Not so much painful as irritating. He pinches at his tear duct, and what he comes up with is ribbed, hard, yellow. The maggot is tossing and bending in his palm, fitful in the atmosphere outside its host's body. Rather than kill it, Justice lets it drop to the floor without much rumination.

From behind, a voice: "You ready, Juss?" It's Graydog.

Justice nods that he is.

Wormbrain takes the stage to the proper introductions, the carefully chosen lights. Out there, these people are pulsing, swarming, like eaters of dead things. Justice will try his damndest to connect with them, though he does not understand why he feels the need to do so. Just as a child does not understand the toll of his own decisions. The permanence. The ephemerality of glory, the retaliative nature of the universe.

Graydog counts off a song, and Justice begins to jam. It is their funkiest, most frenetic tune, with an intro that ebbs and flows for several minutes. Justice brings it rising up and crashing down, and it is, he thinks, the sweetest he has ever played. He is not a fool. He knows what is coming, and he accepts it. He just wishes he would have made it further.

The frontman searches the crowd. The turned-on faces, vibing. Among them is Selene, his broken, ravaged twin sister, robbed of her adulthood. He cannot tell if she is smiling or frowning, maybe neither, for the vile creatures that dress her. She wears the deadest eyes. There is a hand on her shoulder, but it is more of a claw, and it belongs to Smiley. The pale-skinned man is decked out in his usual ensemble, though this time, he has a new accessory: a pocket watch with a chain made of fingerbones. He checks it, shakes his head, deposits it into his vest. Now he is morphing into something even more heinous beside Selene, though nobody seems to notice. His body hunching, arms becoming broad, inward-sloping wings, scored mouth elongating into a hooked beak. A great white vulture, smacking his chops.

"Sometimes it'll come back to take *you*," Selene mouths.

It is time for the first verse. Justice closes his eyes and opens his mouth to sing, and the maggots, too many to count, are bristling from his tongue, pouring from his tongue. And they are falling, falling onto his chest, collectors, falling onto his guitar strings, falling onto the stage in a patter like rainfall. The audience screams and they are falling and Smiley is springing into the air and Justice is very much aware of what is happening to him and he is not aggrieved; no, he is content in this evolutionary process, this price to pay for some measure of transcendence over, among, the devouring forces of the physical world.

About the Author

Matt Starr hails from a town in North Carolina that once gave the world towels, bedsheets, and arguably the most popular NASCAR driver of all time. His debut, *Hell, or High Water*, was published by Main Street Rag in 2018, and his novel, *Prepare to Meet Thy God*, another title from Grinning Skull Press, was released in 2020.

If you liked the stories you've just read, consider checking out *Prepare to Meet Thy God*, which is currently available and can be ordered from your local bookseller.

Chapter One

I didn't think a weekend getaway to the mountains with my girl-friend's friends seemed like all that bad of an idea. It would have to beat the hell out of a sweltering, sticky, and mosquito-plagued summer camp-ing trip to the lake, all of us dehydrated and stinking and sore from sleep-ing on the ground. There was no way it would be any worse than waking up at spring break in Myrtle Beach, breath thick with cigarettes, beer, and dumb words that nobody remembers.

That's what I thought before more than half of us were dead.

We'd all been at the bar shortly after Thanksgiving, and someone, as you often do when you're shitfaced, proposed grand plans—the type that you don't typically follow through with but sound pretty damn good at the time. "We should all go on a skiing trip to the mountains," Beau said. "After New Year's. Martin Luther King weekend or somethin."

Beau was the emotional dad of the group, though he was also one of the youngest: a life-sized teddy bear of a man with sleepy eyes and an easy smile. We all knew that our time and money would be depleted after the holiday season, but Beau had this effortless ability to make things sound like they made all the sense in the world.

"A big group of us," he said. "Just a couple of days. That way, it'll be cheap."

We all agreed—or at least acquiesced—some of us in a more altered state of mind than others. It's hard to say no to most anything at last call. I didn't think much of it for a few weeks after that, but then Willa sent me a text with the link to a rental property everybody was looking at on the HomeAway app. The two-story house was on three hundred acres of land in southeastern West Virginia, a forty-five-minute drive from the Virginia state line and a four-hour road trip from our little townhouse in suburban Durham, North Carolina. It looked like an adequate space for a weekend of drinking, drugs, and belligerent behavior. There was a wraparound porch, a recreation area in the basement, a living room, and six bedrooms—three upstairs, three downstairs—as well as sofas and futons to crash on.

But I was skeptical nonetheless. The trip was going to cost at least a hundred dollars I didn't have, and at the end of the day, the people going were Willa's friends, not mine. The truth is, I didn't have any friends of my own, and even though I'd warmed up to hers since we'd started dating a year and a half before, I still didn't feel like part of the group. Not entirely. I'm sure a lot of it had to do with them being recent college grads and me being a hair shy of thirty years old. I'd had my share of moments with them, but there was still a distance that I couldn't quite put my finger on.

Still, it had been an unseasonably warm winter at home, and the forecast north of us called for lows in the teens. The mountains had always been a place of serenity for me, and I reckoned the cold, tranquil landscape would do me some good. And so it was that when the Friday nine-to-five came and went on the second to last full week of January, I left work, picked out a fifteen-dollar cigar, a nice-ish bottle of wine, and a couple of sixers of beer, and headed for our townhouse, hoping for the best.

Chapter Two

I could hear the patter of Pinto's paws on the hardwood floors from the porch. I opened the door, and our beagle-dachshund mix stretched so hard he could barely keep his footing. He jumped, only once, then retreated into the living room, waiting for me to take my place on the couch. I obliged, and he plopped down on the floor next to me, his bean-shaped body grazing my ankle. My little buddy.

"Good boy, Pinto," I said, fishing for the phone in my jacket pocket. I googled Blue Brier, which was the town we'd have to go through to get to the house, and my search yielded few results. One of them, at least, looked like the town's official website. It had an archaic layout and took forever to load, but when it did, the words "Almost Heaven" popped up in the header. I had a good laugh at that because those words didn't reflect my experience with West Virginia at all. I'd only been there a few times to visit a friend's grandparents, but most of the areas I'd encountered were heavily impoverished and outdated. Looking at the pixelated photos on Blue Brier's website, I didn't have much to convince me otherwise. But I also realized that I probably wasn't being fair.

I started to scroll down when a car horn sounded in the parking lot outside. Pinto yowled and tore off toward the door. Seconds later, Willa entered the townhouse, arms full of grad school books and a tote bag from work. She dropped everything to hug Pinto, who jumped not once or twice, but six or seven times, and I got as jealous as I always did. Pinto was my dog, but Willa was his human.

She rounded the corner. "Hey, baby," she said.

I gave her a good look over. She had been named Willow, but her very Southern grandmother pronounced the second syllable with an "a," and I guess it caught on. She was short, but her heart was big. She was bright, but her eyes were a deep brown. She was quiet, but her smile was loud. I loved her quite a bit.

"Hey," I replied, giving her a hug and a kiss.

Pinto interjected with a woof.

"You packed up?" she asked.

"Pretty much," I said. "When are Mike and Maggie getting here?"

"Soon, I hope. All the couples are gonna get there before us and claim the beds." She laughed nervously. She was anxious like that. "A few people are already there."

"Who?" I asked.

"Beau and Delco, I think. Maybe a few others."

"Delco?" I asked. "Goddammit."

"Heath," Willa said.

Nobody knew what Delco's real name was. He was a transplant from Delaware County, Pennsylvania, and I didn't like him. Everyone else in the friend group did, though—even Beau, and he hated Yankees. Delco was the life of the party and everybody's pal, but I didn't trust him, and I'd always considered myself a pretty good judge of character.

"I just don't understand why he shows up to everything," I said.

"Because he's part of the group. We met him sophomore year, and technically everyone's known him for longer than they've known you."

I went over to the kitchen table and rearranged some of the items in my bookbag, trying to act like what she'd said didn't sting as much as it did.

"You just don't like him because he hit on me that one time."

If there was any truth in that, I wasn't going to acknowledge it. "Well, if he gets out of line and starts hitting walls and shit like he normally does when he's drunk, I'll put him in his place."

"Okay," she said, rolling her eyes.

The doorbell rang, and a patchy-faced, messy-haired guy wearing a gray hoodie pushed into the townhouse. Or maybe the hoodie was wearing him. He nodded at us and said hello to Pinto like he was a person.

"What was the point of ringing the doorbell if you were just gonna come in anyway?" Willa asked him.

"I didn't wanna be rude," Mike said.

Willa rolled her eyes for the second time in as many minutes. "Where's Maggie?" she asked.

"She's right behind me."

"Oh good," Willa said. "Let's go load up the car."

I opened the door, and Maggie stood there on the porch, a jumbled mess of curly red hair and more bags than anyone could possibly need for the weekend. She cut her eyes past me. "Thanks for holding the door for me, Mike."

"You're welcome," he said. Mike and Maggie weren't together, but they squabbled like an old married couple. They couldn't have been much more different from each other than they already were. He was an even-tempered stoner with a predilection toward cheesy jokes. She was a live-wire splayed across the street in the aftermath of a storm.

"Shall we?" I said.

We walked out to Willa's SUV, a new, pearly white crossover she'd just traded her starter car for. And she was proud of it. "Y'all, please be careful when you're putting stuff in," she said. "Lift up, don't drag." She made gestures with her hands like a flight attendant explaining how to activate a flotation device.

I shook my head. "Sooner or later, you're gonna have to lighten up," I warned her, opening the back-left door. I put Pinto's harness on and buckled him in. He responded in typical dramatic fashion.

Mike retrieved his suitcase from his car, and we stacked the hatch of Willa's SUV from floor to roof. As Maggie situated her four bags in the heap, I stepped away. I sized up a capsule in my palm and threw it back without water. There was the slightest head rush as it traced my digestive tract.

"Your medicine?" Willa asked.

I nodded. In a way, I guess it was.

We belted in, and I fired up the engine. Our first stop would be Yadkinville, one hundred miles or so away. Willa's parents had agreed to babysit Pinto for the weekend, and we'd meet them there. The blue hour of the day had just commenced, and we had a long drive ahead of us. Our destination was "Almost Heaven," but the same hellish apprehension I'd wrestled with for most of my life began to hollow itself into my bones. I didn't kick up too much piss about it. How could I? It had been there for as long as I could remember.

Chapter Three

My girlfriend thought I never wanted to hang out with her friends because I was too old and looked down on them as childish and inexperienced. But that wasn't the case. It's true that I sometimes observed their shenanigans through the lens of been-there-done-that, but it was much deeper. I had lost something at their age that I knew I'd never get back. And I was jealous of them because they hadn't.

I was raised by a single mother who busted her ass to make sure I had clothes on my back and food in my stomach. Sometimes the clothes were from a thrift store, and most times, the food was prepared by Stouffer's, but we did the best with what we had. She dragged me along with her to the dentist's office she worked at because she couldn't afford a babysitter. She helped me with my homework every night of the week, even if it meant she had to learn the material herself. If she took a lunch break at all, it was to attend an honor roll that I couldn't have made without her. She cooked and cleaned when she had the time. She mowed the yard.

She was so proud of me when I got into college. But I made it all of three semesters before a lifestyle of partying and the stress of being on my own caught up to me. The transition to college is a pretty big adjustment for anybody, but the growing pains were tenfold for me. I drank and smoked whatever I could get my hands on. Blacked out so many times that there are gaps in my memory that even the most damned ghosts won't haunt. Then one day on a comedown, the emotional toll became too difficult to bear.

I remember that call well:

"Hey, Mama," I'd said.

"Hey, Darlin," she'd replied in her Southern voice— the voice of a woman who'd been brought up in a vernacular house in segregated North Carolina—undoubtedly dropping whatever she was doing to give me every bit of her attention. "What're you doin?"

"Nothing much." I was trying not to cry. I'd been told all my life that men didn't cry. "I'm thinking about coming home."

"For the weekend?"

"No. For good."

There had been a pause. "You ain't thinkin about droppin out, are you?"

"I don't know what I'm thinking about," I'd said. "I just don't feel good."

"What do you mean you don't feel good?"

"I don't feel like I belong. I feel like I'm wasting my time." I'd rarely gotten sick as a child, and when I did, it was serious, so I know she believed me when I said I wasn't well. It wasn't physical this time, but it was no less debilitating.

"All right," she'd said. "Well, you know you can always come home. But I sent you off to school to have a good life."

"I know."

"And I want you to promise me, right here and now," she'd continued, "that if you do this, you'll go back and finish."

"I promise," I'd said. I hadn't meant it, though.